John H. Harding, Jr. presents a powerful verbal portrait of living with insult, pain and anger in the raw, real rural South. From beneath the "pine tree," conversations with "Stack" provide a depth of insight to the best of life in good times and bad. One is moved from laughter to grief, from glory to shame, by the vicarious exposures to life through the extraordinary perceptions of an ordinary man.

T. Wright Morris, Pastor
Shiloh Baptist Church

In 1751, the English poet Thomas Gray visited a county churchyard and penned a lament for all those who lived and died "far from the madding crowd's ignoble strife," their passing marked only by "some frail memorial . . . with uncouth rhymes and shapeless sculpture decked."

Dr. John H. Harding, Jr. has focused on one such individual, a black handyman, farmer and fisherman from Virginia's rural Northern Neck, and erected for him a memorial that will endure. Dr. Harding's reconstructed conversations with Alvin capture a time and place long vanished, but more than that, give us the opportunity to get to know a remarkable man whose voice might otherwise have been lost forever. *Alvin: Recollections and Reflections* is a piece of history and a compelling story.

Ron Carter
Associate Professor of English
Rappahannock Community College

Museums are always seeking authentic artifacts for their collections. Even more sought after are authentic "voices" from the past, the voices that bring life to the material objects. Dr. John H. Harding, Jr. has combined his keen memory and sensitivity for the Virginia of his youth in this new novel, *Alvin: Recollections and Reflections.* This is an artful reconstruction using many conversations with Alvin, a black farmer, cannery worker, menhaden fish boat crewman and soldier. Dr. Harding's descriptions of work on a pre-World War II menhaden fishing steamer are the best that I have read about the day to day lives of these largely black crewmen. The often painful stories about racism that stalked Alvin's progress through life are not muted. By giving voice to this ordinary man, Dr. Harding has created a very special tribute to the qualities of endurance, honesty and dignity that can often be found within the most humble bearers.

R. Angus Murdoch
Director of the Reedville Fishermen's Museum

In his second published novel, Dr. John H. Harding, Jr. once again utilizes the genius of personalized history story telling.

Alvin is a black man who grew up in the rural area of the Northern Neck of Virginia. Through the technique of interviews, Dr. Harding paints a realistic picture of what life was like in the last century for the minority poor and for their families before them.

Personalized historical novels that rely on the recollections of family are a scarce commodity in today's literature. This book offers a rare insight into the lives of blacks in the last century. It's a compelling narrative by a great storyteller.

Richard Maxwell
Freelance writer
Former book reviewer for the *Richmond Times Dispatch*

ALVIN

Recollections and Reflections

Alvin Wormley (courtesy of Ethel Noel)

ALVIN

▼

Recollections and Reflections

John H. Harding, Jr.

To Rick –
John H. Harding Jr

Authors Choice Press

San Jose New York Lincoln Shanghai

Alvin:
Recollections and Reflections

Authors Choice Press
an imprint of iUniverse.com, Inc.

For information address:
iUniverse.com, Inc.
5220 S 16th, Ste. 200
Lincoln, NE 68512
www.iuniverse.com

The stories in this book are fiction although they are based on the real remembrances of Alvin Wormley. Some of the characters retain their real names while others have been changed.

Cover photo courtesy of Robert L. Lunsford.

ISBN: 0-595-18864-8

Printed in the United States of America

To the people of the Northern Neck of Virginia

CONTENTS

▼

ACKNOWLEDGMENTS

▼

I am grateful to the following people for their recollections: Mrs. Maggie Lucas, Mrs. Moses Cockrell, Frissell Flynt, Reverend and Mrs. T. Wright Morris, William and Bessie Hudnall, Alice Dameron, Goldie and Virginia Yerby, Geraldine Jones Toulson, Captain John B. Lowry, Captain H. Urban Haynie, Jefferson Carey, Wilson Jett, Arvell Curry, Magdalene Morris, Miriam Haynie, Robert and Jean McKenney, the Honorable John O. Marsh, Jr., Charles Covington, Mary Bowles, and Clifton Toulson.

I am indebted to Reverend T. Wright Morris, Ron Carter, Angus Murdock, Ada Clark Davis, and Carey Harding for reading my manuscript, and especially to Richard Maxwell for reading and rereading it and making suggestions.

Thanks to Captain John B. Lowry, Fred T. Jett, Warren T. and Lilian Hinton Slaughter, Ethel Noel, Robert L. Lunsford, and the Reedville Fishermen's Museum for the use of their pictures and to Maria Rogers and Winifred Delano for searching their photograph files. Also to Mike Domas for the reproductions of the photographs and to Brenda White Kenner for allowing Mike to photograph her old oak tree.

I give a special thanks to Beth Boon Bradford for her excellent job of editing my manuscript, for her suggestions for ways to make it more readable, and for her encouragement.

My appreciation goes to Jackie Richards for introducing me to iUniverse.com.

Thanks to Suzanne Best for her expertise and knowledge of the details involved in submitting the manuscript for publication. I couldn't have done it without her.

I am deeply grateful to my parents for giving me the opportunity to grow up in this great area of Virginia. Above all, I am indebted to my wife, Karen, who is my typist, my best critic and my best friend.

INTRODUCTION

▼

I have always been interested in oral histories. There was surely no better place to have heard so many stories than the Northern Neck of Virginia. When I was growing up, old timers sat around in the country stores that marked neighborhoods and told their tales. Some were true, but a great many were embellished over time. Many had been told for generations.

Men brought their sons to these gatherings, and my father took me. My father worked with the Marine Resources Commission, so, as a young child, I also had the opportunity to listen to the stories of the people my father visited on the fish docks and oyster shucking houses as part of his job. Later I went with him to hire crew members for the menhaden boats he captained. My experiences visiting neighborhood farms and later working on them, gave me an insight into rural agricultural life before the big changes after World War II.

Needless to say, working in the tomato canning factories and on the menhaden boats during the summers when I was in high school and college offered me the opportunity to see the changes taking place and to hear from those involved how things used to be. Nor shall I discount the many conversations with these same people as patients in my dental office whom I had known since my youth. Many of these people had little earthly wealth but had character and integrity.

The stories in this book are fiction. They are, however, based on the real remembrances of Alvin Wormley, embellished with information garnered by talking to other people in the community. Some of the characters retain their real names while others have been changed. Although Alvin's stories are not presented in his natural dialect, I hope his voice will be heard through my words.

Travel with me down memory lane. See the sights and hear the voices that are no more.

Menhaden fishing boat (courtesy of Robert L. Lunsford)

MENHADEN

The menhaden is an oily fish of the herring family abundantly found along the Atlantic and Gulf Coasts, but usually not harvested for consumption by humans. It is also called moss bunker or bunker. The menhaden feed on plankton and generally swim in large schools near the surface of the water. They have no teeth and are easy prey for flesh-eating fish and fishermen using purse nets. When surrounded the menhaden tend to come to the surface and are easily caught by large nets that have a drawstring at the bottom that can be closed quickly to form a purse. The Indians used the fish to fertilize their crops and taught the settlers to do the same.

Today the menhaden is processed into oil and meal. The oil is used for margarine, soap, paint, varnish, vitamins, linoleum and the tempering of steel. The meal is a high protein product used as an animal feed supplement.

The Northern Neck of Virginia has been the center of the menhaden industry for more than 100 years with numerous processing plants located along the Atlantic and Gulf Coasts. It was an important industry in Alvin's life and in mine.

CHAPTER I

▼

THE FUNERAL

As we stood near the grave, the bugle began to play taps. I looked around at the assembled crowd of friends and relatives. I could see people wiping their eyes, and I was, too. At the bugle's last note, the honor guard fired eight shots into the air. The men in the guard were impressive: Their dress uniforms were smart, their movements precise as they followed the orders of the sergeant in charge.

It was not particularly cold that October day in eastern Virginia although the air was clear and a brisk wind was blowing down from the north. The oaks and maples were giving up their leaves of gold and scarlet, and the dogwood's red berries were in evidence.

Following the rifle salvos, two soldiers folded the American flag that draped the casket and presented it to Alvin Wormley's wife, Myrtle, who continued to sit stoically in her chair beneath the open tent. This act, the passing of the flag, ended the graveside service.

Earlier, Reverend Morris, the minister, had invited all to come into the church building for refreshments. Now, at first slowly and then with a greater sense of purpose, the crowd walked toward the church. The procession was slow as friends and family stopped to greet one another. Some hadn't seen each other for years, and this funeral, like most, was part reunion.

I stopped to speak to Myrtle and to Alvin's brother, Thomas, whom I hadn't seen for fifty years. I told them of my sorrow at their loss, but it was my loss, too. I had enjoyed our many years of friendship, our working together and my visits with Alvin under his pine tree after his retirement.

I was the only white person present at the funeral, but that was not the reason I decided not to go to the reception. I wasn't going because I was drained. Alvin was . . . had been one of my best friends. I missed him, and I needed to remember him alone . . . without the comfort of fried chicken and potato salad.

I would have liked to talk to Alvin's brother. Thomas used to cut grass with a push mower (no motor) at our house. When he was a teenager, I was four or five years old and I always wanted to ride on his back. Thomas was at the services that day, but I knew there would be a large crowd, a lot of talking and noise. I couldn't handle it.

On the way to the church parking lot, I walked slowly, stopping to look at the gravestones of people I had known. The first marked Hilda Lampkin's grave. I remembered the time my dog killed her hens, and all I could do was say I'm sorry and pay for them. Nearby was Uncle Robert Davenport who used to come to cut our hedge. He came in a buggy pulled by a beautiful horse. It was a shiny, high stepping brown horse with four white feet. He wouldn't let me ride the horse, but he often took me for a ride in the buggy. Then there was Matilda Muse who bought apples from me the year my father was terminally ill. These apple sales helped me pay for my college expenses. Alice Jackson had gold front teeth. As a child I asked my mother why I didn't have gold teeth. She told me they were gold caps that covered Mrs. Jackson's own teeth. Next there was Emmanuel Thornton. He had come to me when I was in dental school to see if I would buy a piece of land from him to plant pine trees on, which I did. At the end of the row of gravestones was Reverend Ruffin's stone.

Reverend Ruffin was a former pastor of the church. In the late sixties, as a member of the county school board facing court ordered integration, I spoke to the local ministerial association urging support for the process. Afterwards Reverend Ruffin told me he would do all he could to work toward a peaceful transition. I knew, as a black minister, he had a lot of influence. I'm sure he helped tremendously as we had a smooth passage.

Reverend Morris caught up with me in front of Reverend Ruffin's stone. He thanked me for coming, and again my eyes filled with tears. "I appreciate the service and the nice things you said about Alvin," I said.

His quick response was, "You know they were all true, Doctor Harding. You know as well as anyone." He dropped his gaze, and then he added, "You know we need to enlarge the cemetery. We're running out of room for people like me."

I told him he was certainly right about that. Then, together, we stood looking at the sky, like men have done for hundreds of years. After moments, he said, "Well, it sure doesn't look like rain any time soon, does it?"

We parted company then. He headed for the church building; I continued on my way to my car. There were others who needed to leave just then, too, and the parking lot was crowded. As I waited in line to leave, I thought about the things Reverend Morris had said about Alvin's life. Born in 1912, Alvin was the son of a southern black sharecropper. Without much opportunity of a formal education, he'd taken almost any job, just to help out his family, and later was drafted into a segregated army. Despite the hardships, Alvin had grown up proud and honest. He knew to accept what was offered, and he survived what wasn't. During the service Reverend Morris looked at the crowd and said, "It is much easier growing up black today."

As I crept along, still moving toward the parking lot entrance, I thought about Alvin and I was struck with the sense that I wanted to preserve the things that were most important to his life. I had known him since I was four or five years old. Every year in the spring Alvin raked leaves and cleaned up the fallen branches from the big trees in my parent's yard. He also worked up the flower beds for my mother. When I was grown we took down trees, cut and hauled fire wood, and planted bags of oyster shells in the spring. In the fall we checked them for "spat" (baby oysters) and spread the shells on the oyster ground. One year, Alvin cleaned the underbrush from a lot where we later built a cottage. Every spring he helped me take my wooden boat out of the water to be scraped and painted. No matter the project or the season, whenever we worked together, we did a lot of talking . . . . I will miss that.

CHAPTER 2

▼

MEETING MISS MAGGIE

As the days passed I thought more and more about the things Alvin told me about his life, but I knew very little about his childhood. All of Alvin's brothers and sisters I had known were dead except Thomas. He lived in Baltimore. I didn't think any of Alvin's nieces or nephews could help me with his history. I decided to ask the advice of his niece, Louise Taylor, who lived nearby. After a pleasant conversation with Louise, I told her what I was trying to write. She told me she didn't know much about Alvin's early life. Her mother, Bessie, the oldest child in the family, had died recently. Louise suggested that I contact her aunt, Alvin's sister, Maggie Lucas. I didn't know her, but called her. We talked about my friendship with Alvin, and I told her I wanted to write a book about his life. I asked her to tell me about their life, and her family. Among other things, I wanted to know how they made a living during Alvin's childhood. She seemed delighted. We agreed that I would come to visit her soon. That way we could talk, just one on one. I asked her if she liked fish. "Oh," she exclaimed, "I love fish and seldom can get any here in Warsaw."

Since it was wintertime, I couldn't get any fresh fish either, but I had plenty in our freezer.

My wife agreed to come along and help me take notes. We had no trouble finding her house. The dog in the yard gave a halfhearted bark as we approached the house, and Maggie met us at the door with a warm smile. She was rather short which surprised me, but younger looking than I had pictured when I spoke to her on the phone . . . . I thought she must be ninety, but she had very little gray hair and her eyes were sharp. When I entered the house I presented her with several packages of frozen fish. She seemed thrilled with them. We sat down at the dining room table. She started by asking, "Who are your people at Lilian? That was my childhood home."

"My parents, Jack and Florence Harding, lived at Lilian," I answered.

"I remember them, but, Chile, I'm old and have been gone from there for a long time. You'd better tell me who your grandparents were."

"My grandfather was Jeff Carey," I said.

"Oh, I remember coming to the post office when Mr. Jeff was postmaster. I thought he was the biggest man I had ever seen," she said.

"I thought so, too, when I was a child. He was about six feet four and weighed about three hundred and twenty pounds."

"I remember when your mother was postmaster later, too, and I remember Cap'n Jack, your father and your aunt, Miss Frances," she added.

Maggie asked about many of our mutual friends, both the living and the dead, both black and white. The more we talked the more fascinated I became with this animated black woman who told me, without my asking, that she was eighty-three years old.

I told her I wanted to hear about everything that came to mind, and asked her permission to use a small tape recorder we had brought along.

"I don't mind," she said and after I turned it on she started talking about her childhood. She was younger than Alvin but near his age.

"Our father was Henry Wormley, and our mother was Lena Fleet Wormley. There were nine children born to this union. Alvin was the fourth and I was the sixth. Alvin and I were very close in childhood. I recall when I was just a little girl maybe six years old and Alvin was maybe seven or eight, we worked together in the fields."

I asked about the house they had lived in. Alvin had showed me the remains of it years ago. Even then it was partially fallen in, but I could tell it had been a two-story frame house. There were no outbuildings I could see, only trees almost large enough for timber.

Mrs. Lucas continued. "The house, as I remember, was never painted. There were no screens at the windows, but there were screen doors. There were no partitions in either the upstairs or the downstairs . . . one room upstairs and one downstairs. Momma hung curtains on string to give us some sense of privacy. The inside was not plastered, and there were cracks in the weather boarding we could see through. Momma was always after Daddy about when was he was going to get a deed for the house. This was a constant argument between them. Momma wanted the house to be theirs. He had been promised the house but had never gotten a deed to it. My daddy was a sharecropper. The house was owned by the man he worked for."

She took a deep breath and looked out the window. With her eyes focused on me, she said, "The system of sharecropping then was what came after the war when the black people got their freedom. When the slaves were freed, they had no land, nothing to do. Most of the land was owned by the white people. There were some blacks who were freemen and who owned their own land. This land, as well as their freedom, had been given to them by their former owners, or they had bought the land as well as their freedom. There weren't too many of these people around. There were a lot more poor blacks like my parents whose parents had been slaves."

A young, attractive girl, who looked to be in her late twenties, joined us.

"This is my granddaughter who now lives with me. She works at the school, helping to teach children to read."

"Can I get you all something to drink? Coffee, tea or a soda?" she asked.

"No, thank you, not now, maybe later," I said.

"Okay, I'll leave you to Grandmother. I'll be back later."

Maggie continued, "Well, to get back to sharecropping, the landowner put up the land, furnished the equipment such as it was: plows, disk, harrows, wagons, drill. And, of course, he furnished the horses and mules. Daddy, with the help of his family, had to do all the work which included feeding the horses, cutting and storing hay in the barn, hauling manure and spreading it on the fields. Manure was our major source of fertilizer. The owner did buy some commercial fertilizer for tomatoes. Also, Daddy would make a lime kiln on occasion in winter. The kiln was made up of old stumps and wood piled in the field with oyster shells hauled from a nearby oyster shucking house piled on top. The wood was set afire and burned till the shells dried out and went to pieces. Then he would spread the lime from the shells on the field."

Crossing her arms, Mrs. Lucas exclaimed, "Lordy Chile, what hard work that was! No wonder when my daddy came home at night he didn't have much patience with nine children in the house. We would all be huddled around the kitchen table with a kerosene lamp in the middle, trying to do our homework.

"Momma cooked on a wood cook stove all year long. In the summer it was hot in the house, but in the winter it felt good if you weren't too close to the outside walls. The older boys were the ones to go in the woods and cut wood. We were only allowed to cut dead trees. Of course, they burned better then green wood. In the wintertime, the landowner would let Daddy and the boys cut live trees for the next winter's supply of wood. The deal was that Daddy and the boys cut, split and hauled the wood, then they got half. Before the boys were big enough to help, Momma used to help him with the wood.

"As I think back about my parents, Daddy worked hard, but my momma was the stronger of the two. She was the one who kept the family going. We all worked hard. We did almost anything to make a few pennies."

This didn't surprise me. Maggie Lucas, like all of her family, had worked long hours her whole life, sometimes in a fish house cutting herring, sometimes in a tomato canning factory, and sometimes as somebody's maid.

"At home, everybody got up early. Daddy would build the fire in the wood stove in the summertime. In the wintertime, Momma or Daddy got up in the night two or three times to put wood in the stove to keep the fire from going out. Momma nursed the baby and tended to the other small children with the help of the older girls. It looked like there was always a baby around. The girls helped with breakfast . . . corn cakes or biscuits with molasses and slices of home cured bacon and maybe a fried egg or two apiece. While they cooked the boys helped Daddy feed and water our hogs and chickens and made sure the wood box was full. Alvin always liked to fill the wood box. Also they made sure the two water buckets in the kitchen were filled. Water had to be carried up from the spring back in the woods. After breakfast Daddy went to work on the farm.

"Momma worked as a maid for 'Miss Linda' and her husband, Dr. Covington, who was a dentist. She would walk to their house about a mile away. As I remember she worked about three days a week. Sometimes she didn't eat breakfast with us because she'd cook breakfast for the Covingtons. My father used to say, 'You had better eat something before you go. Your know you have to feed this baby.' We were always glad of the days Momma went to Miss Linda's because she always brought home milk from their cow. We didn't have a cow. On days when Momma and Daddy both were working, one of the older girls had to stay home from school and look after the younger children and keep the fire going. This was true even when she needed to be in school.

"Momma kept a good bunch of hens and two roosters. Do you know anything about a setting hen? Well, every spring the hens want to 'set' on the eggs they lay. Momma would save the best eggs and put about a dozen under the hen in the nest. She didn't want us children to bring in the eggs this time of year. We were too rough. She kept these eggs in the dairy, a small building built up on posts off the ground. It had vents on each side and on the front. Chile, this was our refrigerator! Momma told us Daddy had built it under the trees where it would be in the shade all day. When Momma had enough eggs she would 'set' the hen in a nest she made out of an orange crate from the store. She made a nice nest in the crate, lining one of the sections with pine needles from the woods. The hen would sit on the nest for three weeks getting off at least once a day to get food and water. Momma always had good luck with the eggs hatching because, she said, she was careful with the eggs. Of the chicks that hatched, we used to eat most of the males when they were big enough and save most of the females for laying the next winter. The rest we sold. Alvin and I used to go with Momma to take what chickens there were to sell to Mr. Jackson's store. She would usually buy us some candy, and, of course, Momma would like to look at the dresses. Mr. Jackson would very patiently show her anything she wanted to see. We were much more interested in the candy showcase than anything else in the store."

At this point we were all getting tired of sitting so we decided to take a break. The granddaughter appeared and took our orders for drinks.

CHAPTER 3

▼

MORE FROM MISS MAGGIE

After we got settled again, Mrs. Lucas said, "Let me tell you about working in the fields. After the corn had been planted and was first coming up, the whole family would go into the field to thin it. Momma would put the baby or one of the young children at the edge of field, but not too close to the woods for fear of ticks. Each of us would take a row and pull up the extra plants leaving only two plants in each hill. Daddy carried a hoe and a bag of corn to replant where there was only one plant or none at all in the hill. If any of us broke off a stalk and didn't get it out, Daddy would really get mad. We all carried a short stick that was pointed so if we broke a stalk we could dig down and get it out.

"By the time corn thinning was over, it was time to set the tomato plants. Daddy had grown the plants in a seedbed by planting seed very early in March. He liked to get the plants in the ground by the middle of April, but the plants weren't always ready to transplant by then. When they were ready and the field was worked up and the rows marked off,

Daddy and the older boys would pull the plants up out of the seedbed. Chile, I didn't tell you what a seedbed was, did I?"

"No, but I have an idea," I said.

"Well, you tell me and I'll tell you if you're right."

"Okay," I said, trying to remember the talk at Mr. Jackson's store around the stove in the evening. I knew there was a best way to make a seedbed. "You pick a spot on the south side of some woods where the sun will shine all day long, dig a hole six feet by three feet and two feet deep. Pile the dirt on three sides leaving the south side exposed. On cold nights your plants have to be protected from freezing. Some people use boards with straw on top, or old windows taken from abandon houses."

Mrs. Lucas said with a chuckle, "Well, son, you did pretty good, but you left out a few things. You have to put some well-rotted manure in the pit and some good topsoil on top of that. The manure will give you some heat, and don't forget if it's dry you have got to water your seed to make them grow."

Mrs. Lucas continued, "Daddy and the boys would pull the plants and lay them in bunches in the wagon, wet the roots, and cover them with newspapers or rags. When we got to the field, Daddy would give some of the children handfuls of plants to drop down in the marked off rows while the others would set them out so they were lined up square with the row before. That way they could be worked each way with a cultivator pulled by a horse.

"You see I learned a little bit when I wasn't in school. We had some good teachers. If I had been able to go to school every day I would have learned a lot. But instead of going to school, we had to work. Today too many children get in trouble. We didn't have much time to get in trouble.

"Let me finish telling you about the family working in the fields together. Do you know anything about picking tomatoes?"

"A little," I said.

She went on, "Well, you use five-eighths baskets. That means it's more than half a bushel, and they were heavy when full. It took two of us kids to carry them to the edge of the tomato patch where Daddy and the boys would put them on the wagon to carry to the canning factory. The smaller children used a bucket or pan. When that was filled they carried it to a basket at the edge of the patch. Us older ones would pick two rows at a time putting a basket down in the middle of four plants. If tomatoes were plentiful, we could get a basketful of ripe tomatoes from these four plants. If not too plentiful, we would move the basket to the next four plants.

"When we had picked what Daddy thought was a wagon load of tomatoes, he and the older boys would load them on the wagon and haul them to the tomato canning factory that was about three miles away.

"Daddy would tell us to keep picking, but Momma would usually go to the house to check on the small children or see about lunch. Back then we didn't call it lunch. We called it dinner. I guess it was wrong, but when Momma and Daddy were out of sight, we would go to the nearest shade and sit down. Man, that felt good after picking tomatoes for two hours. We would try to be back in the field before either of them came back. Sometimes Momma and the older girls would stay and fix dinner. This was our big meal of the day.

Pulling fodder and cutting tops
(Library of Congress, Prints and Photographs Division,
FSA-OWI Collection, 1935–1945)

Corn shocks
(Library of Congress, Prints and Photographs Division,
FSA-OWI Collection, 1935–1945)

"About the time school started in September the corn was ready to cut and shock. Daddy and the older boys did most of this, but Momma and all the children helped. Sometimes we would do what they called pulling fodder and cutting tops. We would break off all the leaf blades below the ear and tie a bunch of them to a strong stalk with one of the blades. At the same time the older boys cut the tops of the stalks above the ear and put them in neat stacks. After the corn had been shucked, Daddy would haul in the tops and fodder for feed for the animals.

"When the ears of corn had dried out, we would shuck the ears one stalk at a time. Momma and Daddy and the children all helped. The long and short ears were tossed into separate piles. The short ears were for the pigs, and some were shelled for the chickens. The long ears were for the horses, and the very best ears were saved to grind for cornmeal or seed corn for the next year. Back then they didn't know anything about these hybrid seeds or whatever they call them. The corn stalks were used for feed, or as bedding for the animals. It didn't seem like it was much good for feed. At the end of the day, Daddy or the boys would hitch up the horses to the wagon to haul the corn in from the field. We filled up the basket called a hamper. Nine of these made a barrel. Daddy was always very particular to count them correctly. We got one third of the corn, and the landlord got two thirds.

"Momma always kept two roosters and a nice bunch of hens. We used to carry eggs to the store to get either cash or a 'due bill.' We got more per dozen if we got a 'due bill,' which was a note from the store saying they owed us money, but we had to take it out in trade.

"I'm getting ahead of myself now. Let me finish about the corn.

"Daddy would take a large barrel and a wagon load of corn to the mill each fall to get it ground for cornmeal. Of course, a barrel wouldn't last all winter, but it was a good start. The landlord kept the corn stored in the corn house, and Daddy got it when he needed it. There never was any trouble about measure that I ever heard of between Daddy and the owner. I had heard about other sharecroppers being cut short or thought they were.

"You can see we always had plenty to eat, but the whole family had to work for it. I don't know what people with big families do today if they don't grow some of their own food. We sure did eat good, but we didn't have much money."

Then Mrs. Lucas said, "You all will have to excuse me. It's time for me to take my medicine. This old arthritis can really stove you up."

CHAPTER 4

▼

MISS MAGGIE CONTINUES

Mrs. Lucas returned in a few minutes and said, "What do you want to hear next?"

"Tell me about going to church," I said.

"Oh! That was fun, but those benches got so hard. Sometimes I didn't think the preacher would ever stop. You must remember that we didn't have a car. We used to walk about two miles to church. We didn't leave home until all the morning work was done and dinner was cooked, but not eaten. We didn't eat dinner until we got home from church. We all got dressed up in our best clothes and started the long walk to Shiloh Church. We used to tease Alvin about being so slow getting dressed for church. He walked slowly, too. He was usually the last of our family to get there.

"Sometimes when the weather was bad, we didn't go to church. Instead we looked forward to going to the chapel close to home in the afternoon. It was a small building made of wood, and I don't think it was ever painted. There was a pulpit on a stage at the front and benches with no backs. The benches were in rows on each side of a center aisle. Above the entryway was a steeple with a bell. When there was a funeral at the chapel, they rang the bell once for each year of age of the deceased.

"Every Sunday afternoon the young people used to go to the chapel for their training. This was our Baptist Young Peoples Union meeting. We spoke of it as the BYPU. We were taught to preside and to perform. We learned a lot at these meetings, things we were not taught in school. It was always fun to listen to other children sing and recite but not when you had to do it. I always thought it was a shame that not all the children in the neighborhood came. There wasn't any work done on Sundays, only animals to feed. This was truly our day of rest.

"The pastor was in charge of the training and was the most influential person in the black community followed by the school principal, deacons and teachers. All of these people helped with our training.

"In our case the pastor and the school principal were the same person, Dr. John Ellison. He was a wonderful man. He was interested in the training of black children so they could get better jobs. He was the first principal of the new school built in 1916. It was called the Northumberland Training School; it was a consolidated school. The older children in my family had gone to the Cockrell's Neck School. Alvin and I were proud to go to the new school. Later in life, Dr. Ellison became the president of Virginia Union University.

"I kind of got off the track about going to church. After a long walk to Shiloh the little ones had to go to the toilet. There were two outhouses out back, one for men and boys, one for women and girls. We took care of that in a hurry 'cause we were anxious to see the children of other families. People got to church at different times, most having walked good distances from their homes. We were always glad to see the children, especially in the summertime. Our social life was centered around the church. We might work with and for white people, but we were a segregated society. I remember some of the families who came to church: the Whites, the Thorntons, the Carters, the Taylors, the Toulsons, the Jacksons, the

Haynies, the Lewises, the Williams, the Beas, the Harcums, the Hudnalls, the Cockrells, the Currys.

"Daddy and the other men spent a lot of time talking about their crops, how many barrels of corn per acre they would get, how the tomatoes were turning out, or the need for rain. The menhaden fishermen were always anxious to talk about how they were doing, too. What price were crabs and oysters bringing?

"Every August we had meetings at church. I guess today you would call them revivals, but we called them meetings. These met late afternoon into the evenings and all day on Sunday. These meetings lasted for a week, or sometimes two. Everybody took cooked food. People fried their best chickens for the occasion and took their prize hams from the previous fall. We had deviled eggs and the best bread, the most cakes and pies, and usually watermelon. The men bragged about who had raised the largest melon or whose ham was the biggest. The church was the center of our world.

"The preaching took place every evening. The congregation joined in with 'amens' and 'Praise the Lords.' The week would end with a baptism of the people who had accepted Christ and joined the fellowship of Shiloh Church at the meetings during the week. The baptism was held at the river shore with the minister in the water, the congregation on the banks, and those who had accepted Christ going into the water, one at a time, to be baptized. The people on shore sang and gave thanks to the Lord for the people who had been saved.

"We would save our money for new clothes for the August meetings. They were ordered from Montgomery Ward, Sears and Roebuck and Spiegel catalogs and came C.O.D. Sometimes we ordered early before we had the money. C.O.D.s could stay in the post office for three weeks before they were sent back. If we didn't order in time or found something we liked better at the local store, we just let the package be sent back. We didn't have to pay anything but the two cents postage to mail the order. We bought school clothes and Christmas presents that way, too. We were all so proud of having our own church.

Mrs. Lucas looked me straight in the eye. She said, "We were very proud."

I chimed in, "Mrs. Alice Dameron has told me a lot about how your church got started. I'll tell you what I know. Before the Civil War the blacks had to go to the white churches and sit in the balconies. They had no say in the operation of the church. After the Civil War, thirty-six black men from Fairfields Baptist Church petitioned the Fairfields Baptist Church to separate and form their own church. The petition was accepted, and the first Shiloh Church was built near Gonyon on land donated by a Mr. Blundon, a white man. Later a new, larger church was built. I think that is the present Shiloh near Burgess. Am I right?"

"You are," she said. "You are absolutely correct."

CHAPTER 5

▼

ALVIN'S JOBS

Mrs. Lucas continued, "One of the first jobs Alvin had as a child on the farm was shelling corn. He turned the corn sheller by hand. It was a small machine. The ears of corn were put in a chute on top, one at a time. The empty cobs came out the other end, and the shelled corn came out of the bottom and was caught in a tub. Then it was dumped into bags or in a barrel. Alvin used to say he got the hard job. He turned the sheller while his Daddy and Thomas put ears of corn into the chute. Thomas and Alvin used to switch places, really, and Daddy would fuss with them if they slowed down and the corn cobs got hung up in the sheller. Then they had to stop and clean it out.

Blundon Hinton's Canning Factory (courtesy of Warren T. and Lilian Slaughter)

"Let me tell you about Alvin's first job away from home. It was at the tomato canning factory. He was not very tall, but his shoulders were broad and he was strong. His job was to dump baskets of tomatoes into the washer. From there they would go into the scalder. Then they were put into pans and on to a turntable driven by steam. Women peeling tomatoes would pull off the pans as needed. Then they would peel and core each tomato into a bucket, trying not to leave any peeling. Each worker had a number, and that number was painted on the side of her bucket. When her bucket was filled, she put it on the turntable. Someone else dumped the tomatoes into a long trough. The person who dumped the bucket put a metal token in the bucket. The token was later turned in for pay. When the empty bucket came back on the turntable, the person who had peeled the tomatoes would take out the token and start filling the bucket again.

"This is where I used to work, too. I worked as a little child. I was too short, so I had to stand on a box. When the inspector would come, the owner always told me to hide. I wasn't too young to work, but I was too young to be caught working. My job was to pick out pieces of peeling and any tomatoes that weren't a good color, after the buckets were dumped. Later on, I also peeled tomatoes. So you see Alvin and I worked together at the tomato canning factory, and to us it was a lot of fun.

"Momma and the older girls also worked peeling tomatoes. Most of our working time at the cannery was on the days after we had picked our own tomatoes in our field. When Momma was working with tomatoes she didn't always go to Miss Linda's.

"Daddy used to say that Alvin was the best help at hog killing time. You told me, didn't you, he used to help you?"

"Yes, he did," I said. "Let me tell you about one time."

*   *   *

I had engaged two hogs to be delivered to my home after butchering. Alvin had agreed to help me cut them up, freeze some of the parts and salt the hams and shoulders. The farmer, Mr. King, hadn't let me know when he was going to slaughter the hogs, but one morning he drove up the lane with two dressed hogs in the back of the truck. As it turned out, I was in the hospital for a few days for tests. Well, to make a long story short, my wife, Karen, didn't know what to do with the two hogs, so she called Alvin. In no time at all, he was there, and he took care of the hogs. I called home each night to check on Karen and the little ones. When I asked her what the news was, she said, "Mr. King brought two dead hogs." I thought she said, "two damn hogs." She told me Alvin had butchered all the meat and helped her and my mother salt the "joints." Then the two women made scrapple and liver pudding using the heads, livers and lungs.

*   *   *

Mrs. Lucas smiled. Then she asked if we wanted to stretch our legs and have something to drink.

When we sat down again she said, "I remember one spring when Alvin was about fourteen he got a job at a fish house."

I said, "Yes, Alvin told me about that job."

*   *   *

Fish trapping (courtesy of Fred T. Jett)

During each spring there was a tremendous run of herring in the Chesapeake Bay. The fish were caught by fish trappers who used pound nets strung on polls. These fishermen brought in boatloads of herring, whose roe was prized. At the fish house, the workers would cut the fish's head almost off, and in a single motion open up the stomach to expose the roe that was removed and put into buckets. Then the buckets of roe were dumped into a trough that led to a filling machine. Several women picked over the roe to remove fish scales and other parts of the fish that had no business being mixed with the roe. As it was picked over and pushed down the trough, what one person missed, the next person probably would get out. The trough led to the filling machine. Another person put a salt tablet in each filled can as it passed from the filler to the capping machine. From there the cans were put into metal crates and wheeled to large vats of boiling water. Then the cans were cooked. After they were cooked, they were taken to a warehouse, stacked to cool and dry before being labeled.

Labeling was done on days when there were no fish to cut. The cans of roe were put on a track, by hand, leading to the labeling machine. Alvin told me some of the boys could pick up six cans at a time, but he said he could only pick up four because his fingers were short. The cans would come out of the machine all labeled, but he never could figure out exactly how it worked. This is the same way the tomatoes were canned and labeled in the tomato canning factories.

Alvin told me after the roe was taken out of the herring, the fish were put in wire baskets, washed and dumped in big wooden tanks filled with a strong brine, salt water strong enough to float a potato. He said they used a big wooden rake to stir the fish in the brine several times during the first day, then the fish were drained and washed, and put back in fresh brine again, and again, until the brine was clear. The process took several days. Then the herring were packed in salt in wooden boxes or barrels to be sold in grocery stores.

*   *   *

Miss Maggie looked at me and said, "We worked at any job we could find to make a few dollars. School was important but working came first. It was while working at these jobs that Alvin picked up the nickname 'Stack.' You know his friends and neighbors called him Stack for the rest of his life. I loved all my brothers, Mr. Harding, but Alvin was special to me."

CHAPTER 6

▼

LISTENING TO ALVIN

Through the years, Alvin and I enjoyed many talks, so I knew quite a lot about him by the time he died. I feel I know how he felt about growing up poor, about the Jim Crow laws, and about being in the army. During the many visits I had with Alvin, especially those times we sat under his pine tree during his years of retirement, he told me his thoughts and feelings. Sometimes he talked about things he had probably not thought about in a long time.

A good example of this is when Alvin said, "I want to tell you about the time I stole some candy from Mr. Jackson's store."

I chuckled, but when he began I listened up.

      *   **   **   **

Times had been tight, and my parents didn't have any extra money for us children to buy candy. I had been to the store many times with my momma to take eggs and hens to sell, and I always looked at the candy case really wanting some Mary Janes.

This day Momma told me to wait in the store while she went to the post office across the road. I kinda walked over to the candy showcase on top of the counter and noticed the sliding door on the back of it was open. The Mary Janes were in the back of the showcase. There was an opening in the counter between Mr. Jackson's office and the candy case. The telephone was on the wall near a window in front of me. I wasn't much taller than the counter that held the showcase. When I didn't see anybody around, no clerk, no Mr. Jackson, although there were people on the other side of the store, I stepped behind the counter and reached my hand in the case fearing the phone would ring, but it didn't, and I came out with a handful of Mary Janes. I think they cost five for a penny.

I don't remember how many I got, but as I started to stuff them in my pocket, I turned around, and Mr. Jackson was behind me. He called me by name and said, "Alvin, let me get you a bag," and as he held the bag out, I sheepishly put the candy in it. I didn't know what to say so I said nothing.

Mr. Jackson twisted the bag shut and handed it to me and said, "Next time let me get the candy for you." I handed it back and said, "I don't have any money."

Mr. Jackson laughed and with his big smile said, "That man over there paid for your purchase," as he handed the bag to me.

I hesitated but he insisted that it was my candy. At first, I was afraid to eat any of it, but finally I took one piece out of the bag and was unwrapping it when I saw my momma coming in the door.

She came over to me and said, "Boy, what have you got there?"

She knew I didn't have any money, and I didn't know what Mr. Jackson was going to tell her. I began to think of those seldom used switches she kept in the corner of the kitchen. Mr. Jackson came over to us and asked Momma if he could help her.

She said, "Where did that boy get that candy? I know he didn't have any money," in a very stern voice.

Mr. Jackson gave a big laugh and said, "Someone gave it to him!"

My momma smiled and said, "Mr. Jackson, you are just too much. Yes, sir, you are too much."

Never again did I steal anything. This was a lesson that I never forgot. As we walked home, I opened the bag of candy and held it out for Momma, and she took a piece and I took my second one. I closed the bag and handed it to her and said, "You give the rest of them to the other children." She put her arm around me as she took the bag and hugged me and said with a smile, "You are a good boy."

*   *   *

"I have never told anyone but you about the candy," Alvin said.

CHAPTER 7

▼

ALVIN'S TALES OF MR. JUDSON

The sun was just coming up over the trees. The sky was light yellow with an orange tinge near the horizon. Often watermen referred to this as a red sky, equating this with the saying "red sky in the morning, sailors take warning." But this was a warm July morning with a light breeze from the southwest, and the sky overhead was clear. There had been no dew on the grass or on the car this morning.

As I approached Alvin's house, I saw him cutting grass. I pulled into his drive, and he turned off his lawn mower.

"I fished my gill net this morning and I've brought you all some fish. I hope you want them," I said as I took a bucket from the car.

With a big grin he said, "It's food, ain't it?"

As was typical of Alvin, he added, "Don't cut yourself short." I assured him we had plenty.

He motioned me to a chair in the yard and said, "Take a seat while I put the fish in the refrigerator. I won't clean them until I finish cutting grass."

Alvin soon returned and took a chair next to me under his pine tree. "I can't sleep much these mornings. As soon as it begins to get light, I get up. Hope my lawn mower doesn't wake up my neighbors too much."

*   *   *

As a child growing up on the farm everybody got up early. I remember working corn with a cultivator pulled by a horse. In those days, we really got up early. We ate breakfast in the dark even in the summertime. We didn't know anything about this "fast time" we have now days. The horses were fed and watered and hitched up. I can remember so well putting the muzzle on the horse, so it couldn't eat the corn shoots. The rows of corn were planted checkered so we could work the corn both directions.

We always worked corn barefooted. We had to watch out for potato briars, but we didn't want to ruin our shoes. If we knocked a clod of dirt onto a hill of corn with the cultivator we could often get it off with our bare foot as we were going by without stopping. My brother and I were the ones who usually did the cultivating. We started early in the morning while there was dew on the ground. It was cool and easier on the horses. On hot, dry days the blades of corn hit us on the arms, hands, and feet and felt like they were cutting us, and I guess they were.

I remember one morning I was working corn near the highway. Mr. Judson, a white tenant farmer, was working corn in a field next to ours. I stopped next to the fence, and we exchanged hellos. He and Daddy used to talk a lot and they would help each other. We all worked together at wheat thrashing time.

Mr. Judson was a sight to see. He had on a straw hat, was barefooted, with his pants rolled up to his knees, and he hadn't shaved for some time. About that time a car came along and pulled over and a salesman, or drummer as we called them, got out and asked directions of Mr. Judson.

The drummer remarked, "Your corn looks yellow."

Mr. Judson replied with a straight face, "I planted yellow corn."

The conversation continued. The drummer said, "Because of the poor season you'll probably get only half a crop."

Mr. Judson said, "All I expect is half a crop. The landowner will get the other half."

The drummer turned in disgust and said, "I don't believe you're far from a damn fool."

Mr. Judson looked him straight in the eye and said, "No, there's just a fence between us."

After the drummer left, Mr. Judson turned to me and said, "Don't guess I should have given that fellow a hard time, but I thought he deserved it. These people all dressed up, driving a fancy car, think they know everything. He didn't even know where he wanted to go."

You don't forget the tales Mr. Judson told. I have been to Mr. Jackson's store with my father and heard him go on and on. Momma didn't want Daddy to take me to the store at night because I had to get up and do my chores before I went to school the next day, but most times he took me anyway.

Mr. Jackson had a store that sold everything that anybody would want. It was the center of the community. The post office was across the road. Working men would gather around the coal stove, especially in the wintertime. Mr. Judson was a regular, and I enjoyed hearing him talk about the things he had done. I was never sure he wasn't making some of it up as he went along, but I liked listening all the same.

I remember he told about a time when his father was going to be away. He had told him to sharpen all the tools while he was gone. When Mr. Judson's father came back he asked if he had sharpened the tools.

Mr. Judson said to his father, "Did fine with the axes, chisels and blades, but I couldn't get the gaps out of the hand saw."

Another time he told the tale of how his neighbor, Mr. White, was working corn. He called to Mr. Judson as he was walking by and said, "Come on and tell me a lie while I let the horse cool off."

Mr. Judson, not stopping, said, "Haven't got time; Mr. Coleman fell out of the barn door and broke his leg and I've got to help out."

Mr. White thought to himself, "I've got to go help my neighbor, too." Then Mr. White decided he would take the horse to the barn and follow along to Mr. Coleman's.

Mr. Coleman and Mr. White both got a good laugh out of it, but it was at Mr. White's expense. As you probably guessed, there was no broken leg.

Another man who used to talk a lot at the store was Commodore Keeve. He used to take down trees and cut up wood for people. He called himself a "tree surgeon." At night he would talk about the Bible and answer questions from people in the store. He called himself a preacher, but I always wondered why he didn't preach at my church.

*　　　　*　　　　*

I loved listening to Alvin's tales, but, like always, I knew both of us had to get back to our lives. I stood up.

"Well, Alvin, I have to go to work and you have to finish cutting grass and clean your fish. I'll be back another time to hear some more."

CHAPTER 8

▼

ALVIN'S FIRST FISHING JOB

Alvin's house was on the way to our cottage, and often I saw him sitting in a chair under the pine tree in his yard. If time allowed, I would decide to stop to talk. This particular day we talked about what catches the menhaden boats were getting, and I asked him about his first time on a menhaden boat.

"I remember my dread of asking my daddy if I could go fishing. Daddy had always been a farmer, and didn't think much of working on the water," Alvin said.

       *   *   *

During the winter, I had talked to my neighbor, Johnny Cake Smith, about how I could get a job on a boat. I thought I was old enough to have a job on my own rather than working corn and picking tomatoes with my family. I wasn't sure my parents would let me go on a boat, but as soon as Johnny Cake told me his captain would give me a job on his recommendation, I was delighted.

I decided to wait to tell Momma and Daddy about my job on the menhaden boat until after supper. That evening we were sitting around the kitchen table. The girls were doing the dishes, and Momma was putting away leftover food. The season wouldn't start until the last Monday in May, so I would have plenty of time to help Daddy set tomatoes, get corn planted and thinned, and get the first cutting of hay in the barn. But I wouldn't be there for wheat thrashing which was a busy time and lots of fun.

Daddy was looking at a catalog, and I spoke out real loud and said, "I am going on a fish boat this summer."

I could see the lamp flicker in the middle of the table. The girls stopped washing dishes, and Momma stopped scraping the pans. Daddy looked up. I had no idea what he was going to say. In a low, firm voice he asked me how old I was.

"I'm sixteen," I said slowly.

"What captain is going to take you on a boat?" Daddy asked.

With pride I said, "I have already gotten a job. I'm going with Captain Jim."

"Well, boy, tell me how you got a job on that big steamer?"

All the time Momma just stood with a spoon in one hand and a pan in the other, not taking her eyes off Daddy. Momma might have been the one who held the family together, but these decisions were made by Daddy. I hoped I would get an answer without Momma and Daddy having time to talk it over. My sisters continued to wash dishes but turned so that they were looking first at Daddy, and then at me.

I told Daddy about having talked to our neighbor, Johnny Cake Smith. He had worked on the fishing boats for years and was a drive boatsman. This was about as high up as any black man could go at that time. I had told Johnny Cake that I wanted to go fishing. He had told me he would do what he could for me. I said, "Today he talked to Captain Jim and told him that I was young and strong and would get along with the other crew members and would do what I was told."

Daddy looked down at the catalog he had put on the table and said, "Do you know how much money you will make?"

"Yes, Johnny Cake had said I would get forty-five dollars a month and my board and a bonus of five dollars a month if I stayed the whole season."

"You sure can't make that kind of money on the farm with tomatoes being our money crop, even if you work at an oyster shucking house in the fall for cash," Daddy said.

I told Daddy that with me being away there would be one less mouth to feed.

To my surprise, Daddy looked up at Momma and said, "What do you think?"

Momma pulled a chair from under the table and sat down. She looked at me first, and then at Daddy and said, "You know I don't want him to go. I think about all the men who have been lost off those boats in storms and accidents, and he is so young. I know he will get the hardest work and the dirtiest jobs they have."

Daddy looked at me and said, "You know that don't you, son?"

"Yes," I said. "Johnny Cake has told me this." I was quick to add, "But I can take it."

Momma moved slightly so that the lamp wouldn't block her view of me. She said, "I have a few things to say and I want you to listen carefully. You know your father and I have worked hard all of our lives, and we don't have much to show for it. We don't even own this house, the hovel that it is. I begged your father to try to get a deed to it, so it would belong to us, but it still belongs to the man who owns the farm. All we've got is you children and that is what we have worked so hard for . . . hoping that you would have an easier time than we have had. You know, there isn't much a sixteen-year-old black boy can do with little education. We've tried to get you the best education we could, but there is always too much work to do and work comes before school. I want you to always remember the things we have tried to teach you . . . honesty, always tell the truth, do a good days work and expect to get paid for your efforts. Always remember what the Lord has told you to do, and he will take care of you. Remember to treat the older workers on the boat with respect."

Daddy added, "Most of the crew members have been on boats for years and you are going to get the same pay they get, so you are going to have everyone telling you how to do your job."

I was delighted to get the approval of my parents, and I couldn't wait to tell Johnny Cake. The next morning as soon as breakfast was over, I fed the hogs and filled the wood box, and I hurried to his house.

As I got to the house, the kitchen door swung open. Johnny Cake called out, "What's the trouble?"

"Nothing," I said. "I just wanted to tell you, Daddy said I could go fishing."

"Well, boy, I never saw you move that fast before. Maybe there's hope for you yet," he said.

I could see he was smiling, so I said, "Yes, I was always accused of moving slow, but I always got where I wanted to go."

Johnny Cake held the door open and said, "Come on in." His wife, Nannie Cake asked me if I had had breakfast.

"Yes Ma'am," I said.

"Well, I was sure your momma had fed you. She is always up and going."

Johnny Cake told me to take a chair. I took off my cap and took a seat. Just then his wife said that the wood box was almost empty, and she wanted to make a big kettle of soup for dinner. Dinner was at noon. It was when everyone had their big meal. Johnny Cake took his coat and hat that were hung on a nail on the back of the kitchen door, and I jumped up to help him get a "turn" of wood.

*　　　　　*　　　　　*

During the telling of getting his first grown-up job, I could hear the excitement in Alvin's voice and see the sparkle in his eye.

CHAPTER 9

▼

ALVIN ON THE BOAT

During that spring, Alvin talked to Johnny Cake many times, and he told him what to expect on the boat. Even now the memory of it was fresh in Alvin's mind.

              *   *   *

The crew was made up of the captain, the mate, the pilot, the chief engineer, second engineer, and two firemen, usually all white. The drive boatsman, and the twenty-eight men who handled purse boats and the net were usually all black. Then there was the cook, the assistant cook, and sometimes a member of the crew would help as an extra. These were usually black, too. He wanted to be sure I would get along with the older black crew members who would be sleeping with me in the forepeak (forecastle) which was a dark hole of a compartment between the fish hold and the bow of the boat under the galley. It only had one door. The entrance was down a built-in ladder with a railing. There were two ventilators called air shoots. They usually kept the door to the forepeak open except when it was raining, rough, or cold. There were bunks arranged four high, along the sides and across the back. It was a mass of men . . . about thirty bunks all together. Even with no fish in the hold, the bottom bunk was beneath the water line. A kerosene lantern hung from the ceiling and swung around in rough weather. It had to be filled once or twice a day.

Forepeak (courtesy of Robert L. Lunsford)

Johnny Cake said, "I sleep in a room by myself in the rear of the boat over the engine. The captain, mate and pilot, and any white crew members, sleep in rooms over the galley, behind the wheelhouse off the ship's bridge."

The men in the forepeak slept on straw mattresses with no springs. I soon found out there were chinches (bedbugs) who really "owned the boat" and just allowed us to use the bunks. We served as a food supply for them.

I never knew where they came from, but it seemed to me they were in everyone's clothes, clean or dirty. I'm sure they got taken home and brought back. I wondered who they bit when the boats weren't operating. I tell you they were rank. My first night on board I felt like I was being eaten alive. I asked one of the older men what was biting me, and if he felt anything.

He said, laughing, "Son, ain't you never heard of chinches?"

I said, "No, we don't have them at my house."

Well, he said, "You is lucky."

Johnny Cake also told me about the food. He said it wouldn't be like my momma cooked. We always had plenty of food, and she was a good cook. At sixteen I loved to eat. Johnny Cake told me the company paid for the food, so we wouldn't get the best, but he added, "We'll get plenty of beans, fat back, cabbage, eggs, molasses, and always plenty of good hot biscuits. On Thanksgiving we get turkey and in the fall we get a quarter of beef. Of course, all the good food fish we catch, we eat.

Later he added, "The bunkers (menhaden) we catch usually have a few good fish mixed with them, and I always try to salt a keg or two of them in the fall. They sure do come in handy in the wintertime."

One thing I didn't find out until I was aboard the boat was there wasn't any water for washing in the forepeak. The water came from a spigot on deck piped from a storage tank. We drew water in a bucket and carried it down the ladder to the forepeak. We washed there, and then threw the dirty water overboard. I soon learned not to throw it into the wind. I also learned how dirty I could get sweating after rolling wheelbarrows full of coal to the bunkers of the boat, or pulling the net with oil skins and boots on. Boy, you could really stink! I heard one of the black crew tell a white boy in the crew, "Now you is my color!" That boy was black from the coal dust. Some of the men didn't wash during the entire week, and you can guess how they smelled. There were a couple of older men who gave these fellows a hard time. If they were coming down the ladder to the forepeak, they would trip them and say, "I thought it was a pig coming to the pen."

My biggest surprise was the only way for you to relieve yourself was overboard. We stood near one of the purse boats that was carried above the water on the side of the big boat. While relieving yourself, you could steady yourself by putting a hand on the hull of the purse boat, or you could sit on the railing holding a rope tied to the railing.

My first day on the boat one of the older men in the crew asked me how I got the job. I said, "My neighbor, Johnny Cake, got me the job." He said he was Joshua Cain. He seemed to be a friend of Johnny Cake's, and he told me he would teach me the ropes and look out for me. I'll never forget Mr. Cain's help.

I was one of the men assigned to the ash gang. The job of these men was to hoist buckets of ashes from the fire boxes in the engine room up on deck through a hatch and dump them overboard. Can you imagine dumping ashes with the boat moving and the wind blowing. It wasn't a pretty sight! The ashes would blow in every direction.

Making a set (courtesy of the Reedville Fishermen's Museum)

I remember my first set. The captain, mate, and drive boatsman were up the mast sitting in the crow's nest looking for schools of fish. A school was sighted that the captain thought was worthwhile. He called from the masthead, "In your boats!" In the meantime, the drive boatsman had come down the mast. His drive boat had been put overboard, and he got in it. Standing up, he started to row in order to be in position to be able to drive the school of fish into the net. Now and then, he waved an oar in the direction the fish were moving and hollered something that sounded like, "There they play!" As he was doing this, the two purse boats holding the purse net were lowered from davits on the steamer. Once the boats were in the water, the crew scrambled into their places in them. The captain and the mate came down the masthead, all the while watching the school of fish, and got into the stern of the purse boats. The men with their oars were ready to go. Then the captain said, "Cast off!" and they headed toward the school of fish pointed out by the drive boatsman. Near the fish the purse boats parted at the captain's command, spreading the purse net between them in a circle. Their aim was to enclose the fish. When the purse boats came together at the other side of the school, a purse line through rings on the bottom of the net was passed from one boat to the other. Both purse lines were attached to a "tom" by a snap ring and the tom thrown overboard to close the net at the bottom. Then the purse line was tightened by hand on one of the purse boats referred to as "the big boat." The tom weighed several hundred pounds, because it was usually made of lead. Once the net was together, the tom was brought back into the purse boat. In the meantime, the cork line at the top of the net was pulled by hand into the stern of each purse boat. Once the net was together, the drive boatsman got on the far side of the stretched net and pulled some of the cork line into each side of his boat and secured it. This kept the fish from going over the net and escaping. When the menhaden fish find they are trapped, unlike other fish that swim deeper to try to get away when trapped, they rise to the surface and jump and churn the water, turning it white.

Raising fish (courtesy of Captain John B. Lowry)

Bailing fish (courtesy of Captain John B. Lowry)

The net was pulled into the purse boats so that the fish were pushed into a pocket of the net called "the bunt" which is made of heavier net. Once this was accomplished, the captain called for the steamer to come along side. Then the net between the purse boats was attached to the steamer. A large dip net was lowered into the net to dip the fish into the hold of the boat. While the fish were being dipped, the men in the boats tightened the net to raise the fish. This whole process was called "making a set" and was thrilling. Every fisherman loves to catch fish.

*   *   *

There are big differences, now, in how menhaden fish are caught. The purse boats have engines. The purse line is tightened, and the tom is put overboard and recovered by using a winch. The nets are made of nylon instead of cotton and are longer and deeper. The fish are raised by using a line to the gaff on the mast and pulled by an engine. The fish are taken out of the net using a vacuum hose. The hold of the boat is refrigerated. Today all the boats are diesel, highly mechanized and require a lot fewer men.

CHAPTER 10

▼

ALVIN OYSTERING

On one of my visits with Alvin, I remember asking what experience he'd had working on the water other than working on the fish boat. He told me he "oystered" one winter.

        *   *   *

The job I had on the oyster boat was culling oysters that two men dumped on a cull board. They used tongs that were like two rakes hinged together near the middle of their handles. They would drag the tongs across the bottom and bring up oysters, shells, and other stuff. There was one man on each side of the boat. The cull board was made of several wide boards put together. A ridge along each side kept the oysters on the board. The cull board was laid across the "gunwales" and extended beyond them, so that the water brought up with the oysters would go overboard, and the empty shells could easily be tossed back. I used a piece of metal to break the empty shells and dead oysters from those that were large enough. The good oysters were put in a pile in the bottom of the boat.

When we got to the oyster house, I would shovel the oysters into a big tub. It would be lifted up by a rope and pulley and dumped into a wheelbarrow and taken into the oyster house. By afternoon the oysters caught the previous day had been shucked and packed in gallon and five-gallon cans and shipped to market. The oysters we brought in would be shucked the next day. The oyster shuckers came in early to work, so the oysters could be shucked, packed and shipped by early afternoon. I remember my pay was two dollars a day. I thought I was rich.

I had to be at the boat before sun up. We started work at first light. Seemed like a long time before the last oyster was shoveled into the tub and the boat washed down.

When I was older I worked at an oyster house, hauling shells in a wheelbarrow from the bottom of chutes outside where the oysters shuckers dropped their empty shells. I wheeled the shells to a big pile, laying down boards so I could get high up on the pile. The wind on a cold morning was really cold. The winters then were a lot colder then they are now. Sometimes I would help inside the oyster house, taking wheelbarrows of oysters from the cold storage and putting them on the table in front of the shuckers with a fork.

At that time most of the shuckers were white. Sometimes I got called names if anybody thought he didn't get his fair share of the best oysters. I would always smile and say that was how they came on the shovel from the pile. My boss told me to take the oysters as they came. All the shuckers wanted to shuck the best oysters because they were paid by the gallon, and the better the oysters, the more they could make. A lot of the oysters they get now are from the Gulf of Mexico and are hard to open.

I shucked oysters some, too. When I was a child Daddy used to buy a bushel or two of oysters most every week during the winter. He used to say it was cheap eating. With nine children in the family, it took a lot of food. I would watch Daddy shuck oysters and sometimes he would let me help.

He told me I was a natural. I soon learned to do it as well as he could, but then the job fell mostly to me.

One day when I was about eighteen I was working hauling oysters at the oyster house. The boss asked me if I could shuck oysters. I smiled and said, "Yes, sir." I remember well. It was before Christmas, and there were a lot of orders to fill. One of the shuckers had been sick.

He said, "Let's see what you can do."

Proudly I stepped up to the stall, right in the middle of the white shuckers. The clean bucket was there, but there were no oysters in front of me to shuck.

Several of the shuckers said, "Suppose you want us to bring you your oysters."

"No," I said, "I'll get my own." So I got a wheelbarrow of oysters and put some in front of me and noticed that the man next to me was almost out, so I put the rest of the oysters in front of him. He thanked me. I started to shuck. The boss was standing behind me, watching to see how I was doing. It was very hard not to cut or tear the oyster while prying the shells apart and cutting the oyster loose. I tried to be as careful as I could.

After I had shucked a quart, the boss, Mr. Betts, said, "Boy, I believe you're a natural. You can start shucking tomorrow full time, but today you keep oysters on the table and wheel shells outside. I'll have another man do that tomorrow."

I was so proud of my new job, I could hardly wait to tell Momma and Daddy. When I did, they were proud of me, too.

The next morning when I got to the oyster house, one of the other shuckers was in the stall where I had been the day before. I didn't say anything. The man I had given oysters to was arguing with him, telling him my job was only until the regular shucker came back to work, and I was to shuck in his stall. I told him it was all right, I wouldn't take that stall. The table in front of that stall was against an outside wall where there were windows facing south, and usually gave better light for shucking, even better light than from the light bulbs above the table.

When Mr. Betts came in, he wanted to know what the problem was. Robert, who had taken my stall, said he wanted to shuck there until Barney came back.

Mr. Betts looked at me and said, "Is that all right with you?"

"That's fine," I said.

After Mr. Betts went into his office, Robert said with satisfaction, "I ain't goin' to let no nigger boy have the best light in this oyster house. When Barney comes back he can have his stall, but till then its mine." Some of the shuckers laughed but kept on shucking.

I shucked till the end of the season that year. Barney didn't come back to work at all that winter. I know the white shuckers didn't want black people taking their jobs, but as time went by the white shuckers got better jobs, and the oyster houses were happy to hire black men to shuck. Then as other jobs came along, they hired black women to shuck. Now they can't find many shuckers, and I heard now they bring them in from Mexico. I guess what comes around goes around, or whatever.

                    *   *   *

There was no resentment in his voice.

CHAPTER 11

▼

THE STORM

One August morning a minimal hurricane was forecast to pass nearby. My wife and I had picked a bunch of vegetables and decided to take some to Alvin and Myrtle. As I drove in their drive, I looked at the clouds rolling in. They looked tropical. Alvin came out to greet me, and I gave him the bucket of squash, tomatoes and cucumbers that I brought. He took everything into the house saying he would be right back. When he returned, he insisted that I take a seat in his yard. We talked about the weather and the approach of the hurricane. It was cool that day, even though the sun peeked out of the clouds now and then. No rain yet, but it was predicted. I was in no rush, but I was prepared. I had put extra lines on the boat just in case we had more wind than was expected. The tide was likely to be three to four feet above normal.

Alvin took his seat under the big pine tree. I asked him if he had ever been in a bad storm while he was working on the fish boat.

"Oh, yeah," he said. "It was a bad time I'll never forget."

$*$ $*$ $*$

We had the hold full of fish, and it was getting rougher by the minute. The clouds looked like they do today. I guess it was almost noon. We had eaten dinner some time before. You know we ate dinner about 10 o'clock in the morning. Of course, breakfast was at four in the morning and supper about three in the afternoon. That year I was on a boat fishing out of Lewes, Delaware. When the storm came up, we were fishing up the Jersey coast. We soon took up the purse boats and tied them down. Then the captain hollered from the bridge. "Put the hatch covers on," he said, "and tie them down good. Tie the drive boat down on the hatch covers, now!" We all got the idea that the captain was expecting rough weather. In those days, we didn't get weather reports. As a matter of fact we didn't have a radio on the boat, except the one the cook had in the galley that was run by batteries. The batteries wouldn't last too long in those days. The boat had what they called direct current and a regular radio wouldn't play on it.

I was assistant cook that year, so I spent a lot of time in the galley. I heard a report from one of the New York stations talking about the local weather. They said we would have rain and some wind. We caught our fish that morning near Barnegat Inlet. I thought it would be a long hard trip down the Jersey shore to Delaware Bay. Our plant was just inside the bay on the south shore. I had seen it rough there at the mouth of Delaware Bay before. There's a breakwater right there and you have to come around to the south of it to get to our factory. I knew we would be entering the bay in the dark.

I started working, helping the cook fix supper, but it was hard to cook. The pots didn't want to stay on the stove, although there was a metal edge on the stove to keep the pots from falling on the floor. They slid around on the stove and food spilled when the tops came off. We used coal to fire the stove, and it was my job to keep the fire hot when we cooked. I always tried to keep ahead on my buckets of coal. It was a good thing on this day because we had to keep the doors and the portholes closed to keep the spray from coming in. That made it hot in the galley. I kept thinking it was a long way to Delaware, but nobody said much about it then. We had seen rough weather before, and we had a hold full of fish.

After getting the hatches tied down, the crew headed to the forepeak to catch some sleep before supper. They would probably sleep more after supper, until we got to the factory. Some of them would have to steer their turn or "trick" as they called it, which lasted for an hour. As assistant cook I didn't have to do that. I was anxious to get through with supper so I could catch a nap.

Progress was slow in the galley. The boat would hit a swell and roll to one side or the other, and the metal plates and cups as well as the knives, forks and spoons would go sliding off the table in spite of the ridge around it. I spent a lot of time picking them up off the floor. The cook said he thought the weather was worse, and we should try to eat earlier. He left to go to talk to the captain in the wheelhouse. When he came back he told me he had heard the captain tell the pilot his barometer meant bad weather was coming fast. And he told the cook to have supper as soon as he could get it ready. We hurried and it wasn't long before we had it on the table.

The cook said he was sure some of the men were not going to want to eat. He said some would probably be seasick, or as we used to say, "sea poorly." I had never been seasick, but I had seen other people get "ill sick." I remember one white boy in the crew several years before was sitting on a bag of salt near the stern and one of the crew told him to be careful and to hold onto a rope. He thought a wave might come and wash him overboard. The boy felt so bad he looked up and said, "I hope so."

I looked out of the porthole every now and then and all I could see were dark clouds rolling across the sky. Then, suddenly, it began to rain. It seemed like it was coming down sideways. It was really blowing. Soon the cook told me to ring the bell for supper. I was happy that the squall was over by that time 'cause the bell was outside of the galley. Most of the crew came to eat, and all the officers except the pilot. He would eat when someone relieved him. Nobody wanted much to eat. I remember that much, but I have no recollection of what we ate. I do remember having a hard time trying to stand up and wash the tin plates and cups and the metal utensils. I thought I had good sea legs, but this storm sure put them to the test.

After I finished with the pots and pans, that was my last job after supper, I went to the forepeak and tried to sleep. I had to hold on for fear of being thrown out of bed onto the floor. My bunk was the third from the bottom and I knew I could get hurt if I fell. I decided to get up and go to the galley. As I came out of the forepeak on to the deck the bow of the boat went under, and I was almost washed overboard. I grabbed a rope that was attached to the rigging and held on. As soon as the boat righted itself and the water had gone down the deck I got in the galley as quickly as I could. I wasn't going to wait for the next wave. When I got inside the galley, I was surprised that there were a lot of the men in there. They asked me what I thought. I said I didn't know but it was as rough as I'd ever seen it.

About that time, Ed Jones, the mate came into the galley. We all started to ask him what he thought the storm would do.

"Well," Ed said, "I have seen it rough many times before, specially off the Carolinas, around Cape Hatteras or Frying Pan Shoals. I was on a boat that sank near Cape Hatteras about ten years ago, but that old boat must have lost a plank off the bottom. It was rough, but not this rough, and the pumps couldn't keep ahead of the water. We finally all got in the purse boats and went ashore. No one was hurt or lost. Our biggest problem, as I see it here, is when we come down the coast and get opposite Delaware Bay, it's going to be worse. The tide is bound to be against us. We have to turn into the bay right at the breakwater. That will be our worst time. Our best hope is to get through the worst of the storm before we get there."

One of the men asked, "What about the chances of getting into a harbor along the Jersey coast?"

Ed said, "We might be able to do it if we didn't have a load of fish, but we draw too much water for most of those inlets. I don't blame the captain for not trying it. It's raining hard and will soon be dark. I don't know how big this storm is, but if we haven't seen the worst of it yet, then we're going to have trouble getting to our factory. If we can get around the breakwater we might make it. I'm glad we have a good pilot. If the boat holds together, and he can see anything, he'll be able to get us in safely."

The boat was still taking on big waves, as big or bigger than the one that almost washed me overboard when I was coming to the galley from the forepeak.

Ed said, "We're lucky to have electric lights, so other boats or big ships can see us. In the old days, the waves and wind would have knocked the kerosene lanterns out long ago."

He looked out of the porthole, trying to get a glimpse of the shoreline, and said, "When I came to the galley from the wheelhouse, the rain eased up. I thought we were off Atlantic City, but I'm not sure. I sure would like to be going in Delaware Bay while it's light, but that won't happen."

One of the younger men asked, "What should we do now?"

To our surprise he said, "I want every man to get a life jacket. Put it on now if you want, or have it ready to put on. Get all the men into the galley. Be sure no one is left in the forepeak, and don't bring anything with you. Be sure to wear shoes and *not* rubber boots. I'm going back to the wheelhouse to talk to the captain. I'll tell him what I've asked you to do. There's one other thing I want you all to do. Say a prayer! I don't think this storm is going to lessen, and we'll need all the help we can get."

When the mate left, there was almost a panic in the galley. Grown men started crying; they didn't want to meet their Maker. Just then one of the older men, a long time fisherman and a deacon in my church, called out asking that we listen to him. He stood up in back of the galley, steadying himself with both hands on the ceiling. The rest of us were sitting on benches, holding tight to the galley table.

"We're in a mess, but if we keep our heads, we can make it. Even if the boat sinks. I don't want any of you to think about dying. Think about living. Think about what we can do to help ourselves and each other." He kept talking, telling each man what to do. Then he told two men, Barnes and Smith, to go to the forepeak to get the other men to come to the galley. He thought two men could get from the galley door to the forepeak door better than one. He insisted everyone going on deck put on one of the life preservers stored in the galley. The captain, mate and pilot were in the wheelhouse. They would look after themselves. The cook, engineers, drive boatsman and fireman were either in their quarters at the back of the boat or on duty. There was nothing we could do to help them.

Lucius rapped on the table. "Remember, if we do get in the water, it's not too cold. This is early September, and you're not going to freeze." Pointing to Barnes and Smith, he said, "When you go to the forepeak, tie a line along the deck and rigging for you to hold on to."

I thought that was a good idea. I had almost been washed overboard several hours ago even though it seemed like a week. Everybody was scared. If it hadn't been for Lucius taking charge in the galley, I don't know what the outcome would have been. He was sort of a senior member of the crew, had been on boats for thirty years and was a seine setter. The highest rank of any member of the crew, he was a wise and respected person.

Just then we hit the biggest wave yet. I know the bow came way out of the water. When the boat came down on the other side of the wave, I am sure the pilothouse went under water. Although we held on tight, we were thrown around the galley like metal cups and tin plates.

Lucius asked, "Is everyone all right?" No one said they weren't.

Lucius was standing near me when I got up off the floor, still holding on to the ceiling and hadn't moved. It was then that I decided I was going to stay close to him.

Then he said, "Barnes and Smith, go on deck, get the line up. Cut any of the rigging you have to . . . to get rope."

It was rough. Each wave was breaking over the bow and going down the deck. Lucius kept looking out of the rear galley porthole.

"I'm looking at the hatches. If they stay on, the hold won't fill with water," he said.

It was just about dark and it had stopped raining. When we were on a crest of a wave there were lights visible on the shore. Lucius said it was Ocean City or Cape May.

I could hear him pray under his breath. "It won't be long before we'll be near the breakwater at the mouth of Delaware Bay. Dear God, please let this old crate hold together."

I, too, said a prayer, asking the Lord to save us and any other ships or boats that were caught in the storm.

The men started coming in from the forepeak. Several of them had on boots, and all of them looked real worried. Lucius told them to take the boots off. By this time everyone in the galley had on their life preservers, and those coming in put them on at once.

The galley was crowded, but nobody spoke above a whisper except Lucius. He kept telling the men they would be all right.

"Remember," he said, "if we have to go into the water the life preservers will hold us up. Don't try to climb up on top of anyone. You will just push him down. All you need to do is keep your head above water. Hang on to any piece of wreckage you see or feel in the water. I know most of you can't swim, but you can make it. And if this old boat holds together, we won't have to do any of the things we're talking about. Is everybody here now? We want to be sure!"

Barnes, one of the men Lucius had sent to the forepeak, said, "Linwood was in his bunk. He wouldn't leave. We couldn't make him get up! We even tried pulling him out of his bunk. He held on to the post and said he wasn't leaving his bed. We couldn't think what to do so we left him."

Lucius smiled and said, "He might just be all right."

Just then another wave hit us, this one bigger than the last. Men were tossed like toothpicks all across the galley. Lucius looked out a rear porthole when the boat righted itself. He said he thought one or two hatch covers were gone. The lights on the corners of the engine room were burning, but with the rain and waves, it was hard to see. I asked him if we should try to put the hatch covers back on.

"Put them back on! For heaven's sake, boy, they're gone! Washed overboard!"

I felt kinda foolish, but I wanted to help. Nobody said anything. A few smiled and some kind of laughed.

Then there was a loud thud. It seemed like a wave had hit us broadside and washed over the boat. I could hear Lucius say, "Well, the hold is full of water now . . . . We're getting waves coming down Delaware Bay, so it isn't far to our factory. Maybe we can make it."

The waves kept hitting the side of the boat, and it felt like it would capsize, but it righted itself each time. Lucius said the pumps couldn't pump fast enough to keep the water out of the hold.

Just then Linwood burst into the galley. I don't know how he got out of the forepeak and into the galley door without getting washed overboard even with lines attached along the deck.

Linwood shouted, "The forepeak is filling up with water! Its coming up from the floor." Lucius said, "That means there are some loose boards on the bottom of the boat or the bulkhead between the hold and the forepeak is leaking."

We had no idea about the engine room. If that flooded, we'd have no power. Each wave was breaking over the boat.

At that point Ed appeared at the galley door.

He shouted, "The captain wants everybody to put on a life preserver."

"It's already done and all the men are out of the forepeak," Lucius called out.

"Good," Ed shouted back. "The captain has little or no control of the boat. We'll probably wind up on the breakwater, where the wind and waves would soon break up the boat. Stay where you are now, and if we hit the breakwater, get off the boat as fast as you can. It will probably roll over on it's side and you won't be able to get out of the galley. You men do what Lucius says, and you'll have a good chance of making it."

Just then the lights went out. It was pitch black.

Lucius said, "Keep steady men, its okay."

Then we heard a loud thud, and the boat shuddered and stopped.

The mate hollered, "We're either on shore or on the breakwater!"

The waves kept pounding the boat. Then Ed said, "We've got to get out of the port galley door. The waves are hitting the starboard door too hard. Lucius and I will be the last to leave to be sure everyone gets out okay. We haven't much time. The boat is probably going to turn on its side one way or the other. Get as far away from the boat as you can. You don't want the waves to bang you against the side of the boat."

As bravely as I could, I spoke up, "I'll go first."

"Okay, let's go!" Ed said as he opened the door.

The deck was flooded and water was pouring through the door. I got over the side as quickly as I could, and a wave carried me away from the boat. It was dark, pouring rain, and the waves were huge. At first I could hear men calling out, then their voices became faint. I couldn't swim, but it didn't make any difference. The life jacket held me up, and the waves carried me where they wanted.

All of a sudden the wind stopped blowing, and it stopped raining. I want to tell you, the moon came out! Those of us there in the water saw it. Now they tell us that was the eye of the hurricane we were in, but then they didn't know much about storms. Thank the Good Lord, now they have learned some things to help people who work on the water. We could see the lights on the shore at Cape May and at Lewes, but the thing that caught our attention was our boat. It had rolled over on its side, and the waves were washing over it. The mast was broken off about halfway up. It was a pitiful sight to see. A boat so helpless, and to think, we had just gotten off of it. I called out to the other men in the water, but the only sound I heard was a moan. It kept getting closer. I moved a bit, trying to get closer. At last I saw a person and asked who it was. Not until I touched him did he say anything. He said he was the last man to leave the galley, and the boat had turned over as he came out the door. I knew it was Lucius. He said he had hit his shoulder on something and had no use of his arm and it was hurting a lot. Just then something came floating near us. I reached out and grabbed it. It was part of a hatch cover for the fish hold and it had a rope tied to it. I tied the other end to Lucius's belt and tried to keep his head out of the water.

The water was cold and getting colder. I didn't know how long we could last like this.

Then it started to rain again. The moon disappeared and the wind came up from another direction.

The waves were bigger than ever, and I couldn't tell which way we were drifting. Lucius tried to talk, but all he could say was how much his shoulder hurt. He finally passed out.

The rain came in sheets, stopped, then came again. With the spray from the waves and the torrents of rain, it was hard to see, but I thought I saw a light, maybe Cape Henlopen Lighthouse. It was on our left, so it seemed we were drifting toward the shore. Then suddenly I saw two people on shore. They had flashlights and were shining them into the water. Then one of them called out, "Is anyone there?" I gave a yell! Lucius was unconscious. I tried to paddle, holding on to the hatch cover but it was hard. The wind was blowing the tops off of the waves. I didn't know if the people on shore heard me or not, but I kept calling. The water was beginning to feel warmer to me. Moving helped so I tried to keep paddling, but I was worn out. Eventually, I just drifted. I could hear voices calling, but I couldn't tell where they were. Maybe I was getting more like Lucius.

Suddenly two people appeared in the water right beside me. They stood in the breaking waves holding lights. I tried to call out, but couldn't. But when I felt an arm on my shoulder, I managed a "hello." One of the people grabbed Lucius, and the other took hold of me. They dragged us to the shore and up the beach. I couldn't walk. I couldn't even stand. They wrapped us in blankets and gave us hot coffee to drink. It tasted good.

One of our rescuers said, "We're going to take this man to the hospital and you will follow in another car."

I asked if they had found any other men from the crew. They said, "No, but we hear that a Coast Guard cutter picked up some of the men, and they were all right. Others are still out looking."

At the hospital they checked me out, and I was okay. Someone along the way had given me some dry clothes. They didn't fit too good, but they felt better than that blanket over my wet clothes. I asked about Lucius. They told me he was having surgery for a broken shoulder and would be all right. They told me twelve men had been picked up so far. They also told me that the storm was over.

One of the men who pulled us out of the bay offered to take me to the fish factory. I said I would be glad to go as I had nowhere else to go and no money. I was just glad to be alive. They found a place for me to sleep at the factory, and I must have slept for a day and a half. When I finally woke up, someone told me to come to supper at the cookhouse. Boy, was I hungry. A bunch of men from the boat were eating supper. I wanted to know about the others. They told me some of the men hadn't been found, but they knew three were dead including the captain who had been smashed against the rocks when the boat turned over.

As I started to eat, Linwood walked in. He was sure excited. The company had said they would give us $10 each and a bus ticket home. Sure didn't seem like much, losing all our clothes, boots and oilskins, but what could we do? I started thinking about a job. I could help Daddy cut corn, but I was hoping to get a job at the oyster house. All the while I shoveled in cabbage, red meat and hot biscuits.

▼

CHAPTER 12

ALVIN GOES IN THE ARMY

One spring I went by Alvin's house and got him to help me pull up my boat so I could clean it and paint it. Once it was out of the water, we put a rope around the middle of the boat and turned it over by attaching Alvin's block and tackle to the crotch of a tree above the boat. We always leaned the boat against the tree so when the paint on the bottom was dry, I could lower it down by myself and paint the inside and the outsides of the boat. I used copper paint on the bottom primarily to keep the worms out. Without that copper it would probably have been rotten after a year. I only pulled the boat out once a year, so I tried to do a thorough job. By that I mean, hosed off the boat, cleaned off any barnacles, chipped off loose paint and renailed when necessary.

Alvin thoroughly enjoyed tying the necessary knots and pulling the boat out of the water, but he left the rest to me. On this particular day though, Alvin picked up a paint scrapper and began to work with me on the bottom of the boat. The weather was hot. It must have been 100 degrees, and we both got pretty sweaty, so when the boat was clean we sat on the bench out on the dock. It was afternoon and the trees provided some shade.

"Were you in the army or navy?" he asked. It was assumed that people my age had been in some branch of the service.

"I spent two years in the army at the end of the Korean Conflict," I replied. Alvin said, "I spent two years in the army during World War II."

Alvin kept asking me questions about the army, what I did, where I was stationed, but I got the feeling he wanted to tell me about his life in the army. I said, "Alvin, please tell me about your experience, I'd love to hear it."

He began by telling me he hadn't ever talked much about his time in the army. Then he looked at me. "Would you like to hear about it, about the good times and the not so good?"

"Sure," I said.

*   *   *

Well, it was January 1943 when I went for my physical exam. They told me I passed, but it wasn't much of an exam. It seemed like if you had two arms, two legs, and could walk and see, you passed. Anyway, I was told to report to the draft board office in Heathsville in a couple of weeks. From there we took a bus to Richmond to what they called an induction center. There we had to take an oath. Then they gave us a tag and some papers and told us which bus to get on. While we waited for the buses to come, they gave us a good lunch. We spent time looking at each other's tags to see where everyone was going. All the boys I came with were going to different places.

When the time came to leave, I found my bus and got on. I didn't see anyone I had ever seen before. The man in charge of us told us we were going to Fort Lee near Petersburg. It seemed like no time after we left the Richmond city limits that we were going through the gate at Fort Lee. At the gate the guards with guns waved us on through. Inside the gate we stopped. The man in charge got out and made a phone call. He got back on the bus and told the driver where to go. It had been cloudy all day and now it began to rain. The guards were checking the papers of each car coming and going. I felt like I was going to prison. It was a bad feeling. It felt like the bottom was falling out of my stomach and my legs ached something awful.

There were buildings everywhere. As the bus drove along, I tried to count them, but they went by too fast. Most of them had two floors, but some one-story buildings were scattered among them. They all looked new, and the area around them was kept very neat. There were men everywhere in long lines waiting to go into the buildings and groups of men were marching from one place to another.

Our bus stopped outside one of these buildings, and our leader announced that this building was our new home. He told us to stand outside and wait until our sergeant came to show us where to go. By the time we got off the bus, the rain had stopped. All I had with me was an old suitcase with a few items in it like a razor and the best clothes that I had. We had been told to bring just a few things, but they didn't tell us what. As we stood in a group talking to each other, everyone was saying, "What's your name?" and "Where are you from?" It was not until then that I realized that all of us were black. Pretty soon a white sergeant came along and told us to line up by height in two rows. There was a big shuffle, but we did it pretty well. He had some of us change places. The first half of each row was told to go upstairs, the rest to the first floor. When I went into the building on the first floor I saw two lines of double-decker beds along each side of the building. The sergeant told us to put our suitcase or bag on the bed, and then stand in front of the beds.

Then a black sergeant came in. He announced, "My name is Sergeant Brown. I am going to make soldiers out of you, whether you like it or not. I am going to be your mother, father, teacher, preacher. I've been in the army thirty years and was ready to retire when this war started. This first part of training will last for eight weeks. You will have no leave and no passes until you have proven yourselves."

Another soldier came in. The sergeant said, "This is my assistant, Corporal Yamaki, a Japanese American born in Washington state. You will meet your commanding officer, Captain Butler," he added. "Tomorrow you will get your clothes, your I.D. card and your shots and equipment. Tonight you will eat supper in the mess hall next door. Without an I.D. card you should not leave these two buildings. Breakfast will be at 5:00 A.M. sharp. Get a good night's sleep. Tomorrow and every day thereafter will be rough. I assure you your training will be rough, but tonight you can just relax. Does anyone have a question?"

One of the fellows put up his hand, "What is our address? I want to write to my mother."

He gave us our address. As a matter of fact he had it posted on the bulletin board. This was when I first knew I was in the Quartermaster Corp. The trouble was, I didn't know what that was.

At 4:30 the next morning, Sergeant Brown came running into the barracks and told us to get up. Those who were slow soon found out he meant it. He turned their beds over and said, "When I tell you to do something, I expect you to do it. Now!"

That first full day I remember well, getting all new clothes, shoes and uniforms that fit. Pictures were taken for an I.D. card. It wasn't too long before we found out how important that I.D. card was. Most places we went, we had to show it to someone.

We were taught all kinds of things, how to stand at attention, how to salute, and who to salute. We marched everywhere we went. The field drilling was constant, so many right faces, left faces and about faces. A lot of men got mixed up.

Sergeant Brown kept saying, "You will keep doing it until you get it right!"

We were soon assigned rifles and taught how to care for them. We marched with them and spent time on the rifle range. We learned how to pack our backpacks. Fifteen-mile hikes before breakfast were common. Sometimes we marched at quick time. I felt sorry for those city boys; they got so tired.

I remember one night I was on guard duty sitting in the orderly room with Corporal Yamaki. It was hard for me to say his name. I just called him Corporal.

The corporal said, "Do you mind talking to me about how it feels to be a colored American?"

"Ask anything you want. It's all right with me. I'll give you the best answer I can," I said.

"Well," he started, "How does it feel to see signs that say 'Whites Only' or 'Colored Eating Areas' or 'Colored Waiting Rooms'? Just explain this to me. Here we are supposed to be fighting for our country and you, by law, have to ride in the back of a bus. And my family is in a camp someplace in eastern Washington State because Japan and the United States are at war. They are Japanese Americans. Both my parents were born in the United States. I assume you, too, were born in this country. I spent nine months in that camp. I'll tell you about it later, but I want to know how you feel about the way you're treated because you're colored."

"Well," I said softly, "I've really never given it much thought. I just took things like they were. My parents were born free, but my grandparents were slaves. I figured I was better off then they were. Growing up when I rode the bus and sat in the back of the bus with all the other colored people, I didn't know it was a law. Let me tell you about the time I went to Florida with five other men to pick up a fish boat and bring it to Reedville."

"I wasn't doing much that spring, just waiting to go fishing. This job paid good. There were five of us black men in the crew and the captain, who was doing the driving. None of us could drive. We had no problem until we stopped to get gas and go to the bathroom. The service station owner said they had no bathrooms for 'coloreds,' just for whites only. The bathroom problem was easily solved. We stopped by the side of the road and went into the woods. Next, we stopped at a lunchroom. The captain told us to stay close, and he would check inside. He was gone a long time, but he came back with a big box of sandwiches and some bottles of soda.

"We had to stop often for gas, and it felt good to get out of the car. There were, like I said, six of us in the car . . . three in the front and three in the back. I always seemed to get in the middle. My legs kept getting cramped. Some of the men smoked all the time and I didn't. I was glad we could keep the windows rolled down.

"It was 1938. I had never been south except to North Carolina fishing. I spent most of the time then on the boat or at a black lunchroom. I had been on fish boats going north. Once we tied up at the Brooklyn Navy Yard, and some of us went to see the big city by subway. I had also fished in Delaware several years. The big difference in being in the north and the south was this: The south had all these rules and you knew where you stood. But in the north there were unwritten laws. I remember going into a restaurant in New York and wanting a sandwich. They told me they didn't serve my color. I remember, I could hardly understand what that person said, but I left without saying anything. I thought, why did this person have the right to turn me down when I wanted to buy food, and he could hardly speak English.

"On our trip south in 1938, I felt sorry for our captain. He tried to get us meals. We were all tired, and it was hot in South Carolina and Georgia in May. It must have been about 4 o'clock in the morning when the captain said he was going to pull over and get a short nap. All the rest of us had been asleep off and on all night. We all got out of the car, and the captain went right to sleep. We walked around and found there was a field on the left side of the road. Everyone used it as a toilet. It was a cool morning. You could see the bright red sky in the east before the sun came up. The captain slept about two hours. Then we were on our way again. It wasn't too long before we saw a sign that said, 'Entering Florida.' I thought the captain was waiting until we got into Florida to stop for something to eat. Maybe the rules weren't as strict there.

"We had the same problem getting breakfast. The captain asked in the restaurant about feeding the men. He said we were driving from Virginia to Fernandina, Florida, to pick up a fish boat. The restaurant owner was very friendly to the captain and told him that he would fix each of us a tray if we would eat outside. The food was good, as I remember, eggs, bacon and hot cakes. I was tired of sandwiches. The company had given the captain money to pay for our meals. By lunchtime we were in Fernandina and on the boat. One of the men with us was the cook. They had already put the grub on the boat for the trip north, and he went to work fixing dinner."

The corporal leaned back in his chair with his hands behind his head and said, "I see . . . . I, too, have not been treated like I think all Americans should be treated. After all, what are we fighting for? I'm going to get us a cup of coffee and when I get back I'm going to tell you about my family's experience."

*   *   *

Alvin said, "I had never thought about this before. Now I was going to fight for my country. That man sure opened my eyes!"

CHAPTER 13

▼

CORPORAL YAMAKI'S STORY

Corporal Yamaki soon returned with two cups of coffee. I wasn't much of a cof-fee drinker, but when I had to be up most of the night, it helped me stay awake. The corporal sat in his chair; he seemed to really enjoy his coffee.

Then he said, "I'm going to tell you how my family and I have been treated. It's not like your experience, but it is ugly just the same."

* * *

Both my parents were born in Washington State. They graduated from high school and were married just after they finished school. My grand-parents, who were born in Japan, acquired a small farm in the Puyallup Valley, a very fertile area with plenty of rain. They had both worked for other farmers and bought the land by paying a little each month. The land's timber had been cut, and there wasn't much there but stumps and brush. They cleared the land by hand, with the help of a mule, after put-ting in a day's work on another farm. They spent all of their spare time clearing the land and moving rocks. My grandfather on my mother's side was one of the first to raise tulips in the area. He didn't sell the tulips while they were blooming, but he sold the bulbs, which was more profitable. It wasn't long before the area became quite a flower growing place. My grandparents didn't get rich, but they were able to make a good living by hard work.

Both my parents worked with the flowers and bulbs, but they wanted me to go to college. I had hoped to go to college and then to medical school, but the war came along. Now there is little chance I will be able to go when the war is over.

As you know, Japan attacked the United States in 1941. After the attack on Pearl Harbor, every time we went to town to buy anything we got such awful looks and I could see hate in people's eyes. The people we thought were friends, those I had gone to school with, barely spoke. Sometimes as I passed, I could hear someone say "dirty Jap."

As I said before, both of my parents were born in this country. My grandparents, who came from Japan, were dead. We didn't know anyone in Japan.

My father came home one day all upset. He had been to the post office and was told that his mail had been opened by the FBI. He asked what they were looking for. The man said he didn't know, but all the mail of Japanese people was being opened. This really got my father upset. He knew the man working in the post office was German, and he had come to this country after the first World War. My father asked why his mail wasn't opened. The next day two FBI agents came to the house and talked to my parents.

I was told these things later. At the time I was away. I was a junior in college and didn't get home until almost Christmas. It was just before exams, and most of the students I was associated with were so involved in finishing their organic chemistry and comparative anatomy, there was little time to do any more than listen to the news on the radio.

When I got home from school, there was mass hysteria. I didn't know what to think or what to believe. My parents were so anxious, and rumors were traveling fast. My father told me to stay home in January until all this got sorted out.

I couldn't believe what was happening. I considered myself as good an American as anybody. I surely did not approve of what Japan was doing. I even thought of joining the army. In early January, we got notice that we would be detained and taken to a camp somewhere. We had only three days notice.

I was the oldest child. I have a younger brother and there are three girls between us. Needless to say we were all upset. My father was beside himself. He had a good business. Germany now controlled Holland, so the bulb sales in the U.S. were booming. There was no one to take over the business. All of the employees were Japanese Americans, and they were all going to be put in camps.

A neighbor, who also had a flower farm but raised bulbs like my father, came to him the next day and offered to buy his farm. My father did not want to sell, but with no one to tend to the bulbs, they would soon be worthless. He thought the offer was fair. The offer did not include the sorting machines and tractors or household items. Since we had been told we could take only one suitcase per person, these things would have to be sold for what we could get for them or left. That night my father walked the floor. Next morning he said he didn't see anything else to do but sell the farm. We had no idea how long we would be in the camp or where the camp would be. The whole Japanese community was in a quandary. There wasn't just a lack of information . . . there was no information!

The war news was bad. The Japanese were capturing islands in the Pacific almost at will. Would they invade the U.S. mainland? Who would have thought they would bomb the Hawaiian Islands?

Mother kept the other children home from school after Christmas vacation. The younger ones told her tales of being pushed and shoved and called a "dirty Jap." Mother decided we should stick together and do what Father said was best.

Mother's brother, who now owned the farm she was raised on, visited us the night before to say he was going to sell his farm. The best offer he received was only half of its value. They talked about how hard their parents had worked to clear the land of stumps and rocks and to raise flowers.

Father came out of the bedroom with a smile on his face, bent over, and kissed Mother on the forehead, and said softly, "I think we had better sell. There might not be anything here when we get back. Mother, pack each suitcase. Include in each one some of our family dishes or some bowls. We should keep something of our culture if we can. Everything else we will put in the sheds to be sold. I will go now to tell our neighbor I'm going to take his offer for the farm. When I get back I want all of us to take a walk around the farm to look at the fields one last time, and remember how my parents worked and how I worked as a young child trying to help. Many times I held the rope tied to the harness of the mule and got him to pull on a stump or root my father had hooked with a chain. I want you to see the ditches they dug by hand and the old lean-to shed they called home before a permanent house was built."

My father asked me to go with him. As we drove along he told me he had hoped to be able to give our place to his children or his children's children, but it was not to be.

As we approached Mr. Johansen's house, we saw him and his wife sitting on the porch. They were both from Norway and had real blonde hair that was beginning to turn gray. Their three children were grown and working in an aircraft factory in Seattle. His farm was small enough that he and his wife did all the work except at picking time and bulb digging time when local people were hired to help. I had worked for them parts of several summers after our work was done. They were both very nice. As we came down their lane, my father said, "I would rather sell to these people than any of our other neighbors."

The Johansens seemed glad to see us and told us again and again they didn't understand what was happening or why it was happening. Mr. Johansen said, "You are law abiding citizens. You pay your taxes, and you don't bother anybody."

Then my father told Mr. Johansen he had decided to take his offer. They decided on an attorney to use and on some other details. From there we went to the lawyer's office so he could draw up the necessary papers. Before we went home we stopped at the general store where we bought our supplies. We told the owner, Mr. Levin, we were having a sale of our equipment and furniture the next day.

"I sure am sorry about what's happening," the storekeeper said. "Another neighbor, Mr. Kimura, had a sale and got little or nothing for his things. I know your equipment is in good shape. If you don't get a fair price for it, I'll store it and sell it in the spring. January isn't a good time to sell equipment."

My father thanked him for everything and added, "We'll see how the sale goes."

They shook hands and Mr. Levin said, "I will call people I know who might be interested in the equipment and tell people who come into the store."

Driving home, Daddy seemed sad but relieved. "We must get the equipment and furniture into the sorting sheds tonight."

After supper we all walked along the edges of the fields looking at the long rows of tulips and daffodils Daddy had helped his father plant. We all remembered how hard we had worked in these fields. I could see sadness in my father's eyes and tears on his cheeks as he talked about different parts of the farm. There was mist on his glasses, but he didn't wipe them. The sky was cloudy. This was the kind of weather we had most of the winter, not much hard rain, but light mist most of the time with a shower now and then.

When we returned from our walk, we moved equipment around in the sorting sheds and set up tables to put our household items on. Mother and the younger children had packed most things in boxes. We carried box after box of clothes and dishes, pots and pans, and toys to the tables. My younger sisters wanted to keep all their toys, but Mother said they could keep only one toy. She told them to pick out the one they wanted most.

The next morning a lot of people came to look at the things we had for sale. Daddy had thought it would be better not to put prices on items, but to see what we were offered. Some of the people looked at our things with scorn.

I heard one man say, "I don't want anything any dirty Jap has had his hands on."

We sold a few items, but very few. The prices offered were nothing.

One lady said, "Why buy them now? They can't take them with them." And she was so right.

I guess if other Japanese Americans had been at the sale, it would have been different, but they were in the same boat. Mr. Johansen told my father to put our things in one corner of the shed, and he would try to sell them in the spring. He said he would send us the money. No one even offered to buy the equipment, so it was good that the storekeeper, Mr. Levin, was going to take it.

The next day, our last day, we finished our packing. Mother asked Father about the food. He said, "After breakfast, pack a good lunch. Anything that is canned, leave in the house, anything else throw out."

We were at the bus station early with a lot of our neighbors and friends. What really hit us was the number of soldiers and police with guns who were standing around. A man who identified himself as an FBI agent told us families would stay together. He said we were going to a camp, but he didn't say where. None of our people talked. They seemed resigned.

When the buses came, they were army buses. We were told to get on as our names were called.

Mother said, "Stay close and don't talk."

All of the bags were searched by the soldiers, but nothing was removed. When he came to my bag, I asked the soldier what he was looking for. He said, "Man, weapons! You know we can't trust you Japs!" I wanted to knock his teeth in but I didn't. Here I was, a young man accomplished with three and a half years of premed in college, and I had to listen to such talk.

We headed east. We couldn't see Mt. Rainier for the clouds. It was misting. I told my younger brother we would soon be going through the mountain pass, heading for eastern Washington. As we got into the mountains, the mist changed to snow. I heard Mother say she was glad we had worn our warmest clothes and our heavy coats.

"Just the sight of snow makes me cold," she whispered to Father.

Our bus pulled into a parking lot after we got through the pass and out of the high mountains. The snow stopped. We could see broken clouds with glimpses of the sun. We were fed lunch from an army truck at the far end of the parking lot. Soldiers served cold unappetizing food on metal trays.

One of our group asked a guard about bathroom facilities we could use.

"If you have to go, go in the woods. That's what Japs do, isn't it?" he said. He laughed.

Men and boys went in one direction, and women and children in another. When we came out of the woods, two other buses were pulling into the parking lot. I knew what was in store for them.

It wasn't long before we were on our way again through the desolate countryside. It was almost like desert. Most of the people on the bus had never seen this type of terrain. I had been to school with a boy from Spokane who had talked about this kind of country. I kept reading the road signs and felt sure we were heading toward Spokane. Two guards with pistols on their sides sat on the front seats of the bus. They kept laughing and telling people close to them how they were going to take care of the Japs. I thought I knew how they felt . . . . Maybe they had friends killed in the Pacific. But these Japanese Americans on the bus had done nothing wrong. We were American citizens as much as the Germans, Italians or Norwegians who were our neighbors. All kinds of thoughts ran through my mind about how I would get even or run away.

We stopped twice during the afternoon to relieve ourselves behind bushes on either side of the road. It was almost dark when we turned off the main highway. Soon I could see buildings in the distance. Later we found out this had been an old C.C.C. camp from the depression era. It had not been used in years. It was constructed as a temporary facility when it was built, but high newly-constructed barbed wire fences were much in evidence.

When we got out of the bus, a sergeant said, "There will be four families in each building, two up and two down. There is a bathroom on the first floor of each building. There are no partitions, but you Japs will have to make do. Food will be brought to you tomorrow. Each family will have to do its own cooking, but you will be fed tonight."

The Hitosaki family was on our floor. We knew them, though not well. They were nice, but with five children, two older boys and three younger girls near the age of my sisters, it would be crowded. Mr. Hitosaki had a cherry farm not far from us. He and my father spent a lot of time talking about what to do and what had happened. Mr. Hitosaki was forced to sell his farm, too. He said the trees needed care and there was no one to do it. Most of the families had sold their farms not knowing if or when they would get back to them. They also worried the government might confiscate their money. Everything was so uncertain.

There was nothing to do around the camps. I read what books I could get my hands on and talked to other men my age. I helped my mother and sisters put up sheets for partitions. It was so depressing to see my father as he withdrew into his shell. I tried to cheer him up, but it was hopeless. We were in the camp because we were of Japanese ancestry although we were American citizens.

The food we were given was army issue and not very good. We were not used to eating dehydrated potatoes and eggs and drinking powered milk, but I never heard of anyone going hungry. We couldn't have a radio because of the fear we would send and receive messages from Japanese submarines. I don't know how we could have done that.

In the late spring I talked to other men my age as we did our morning and afternoon walks around the compound. I heard that someone was coming from the army to ask us to enlist. We would be full-fledged American soldiers. I laughed when I heard that. I would go from being held in a camp under guard to being an American soldier. I couldn't believe it! As I remember, the next week I saw a poster. It said an army recruiter was coming to talk to anyone who wanted to enlist. Some of my new friends at the camp decided they wanted to enlist. They saw no other opportunity to leave the camp.

I decided to talk to my father about joining the army. He looked sadly at me and said, "Son, there is no hope for me and your mother. I don't know what they will do with us, but you are young. Your life is ahead of you. I had hoped you would become a doctor or at least run the business. The government has basically taken our land and business, and you know we didn't get much for it. I am afraid you will have to be on your own, but you will also have to look out for the family. You see I can't do anything. I have worked all my life, and now here I sit with nothing to do. All I have are my memories."

Well, the army recruiter came to talk, and most of the eligible young men joined the army. So here I am. My family is still in that camp eating dried potatoes and eggs and drinking powdered milk.

*　　　　　*　　　　　*

As the corporal downed the last of his cold coffee, I looked at his face and saw tears in his eyes. I tried to think of something to say. "You have done well in the army so far. I bet one day you'll be a general."

He smiled and said, "You know those tests we took when we came into the army?

"Yeah," I said, "I could hardly read some of the questions."

"Well, I got them all right. So after basic training they made me an instructor. Your group is the seventh group I have been with."

I asked him where he thought I would go after basic training was over.

"You will probably go to some school for your next phase of training, but it will be in the Quartermaster Corp. There are all kinds of schools right here at Fort Lee. Since you have worked on a boat, they could put you loading or unloading ships any place in the world. You know the army will put you where you are needed."

Corporal Yamaki looked at the clock on the wall and told me that I could go on to bed. My relief would be there any minute.

CHAPTER 14

▼

ALVIN GOES TO EUROPE

"Well," I told Alvin, "you sure seemed to have made a friend in your company."

"Yeah, but I never saw him after basic training. Since then, I've often thought about how he and his family were treated."

As Alvin seemed anxious to talk about his army experience, I was anxious for him to keep on talking. "What happened to you after basic training?"

Alvin started to say something, but instead pointed at the pond. "See there, a fish jumped clean, clear out of the water."

I hadn't seen the fish. I kept watching the expression on Alvin's face. I thought he was toying with telling me things he hadn't thought about in a long time. Maybe I was prying into his mind; just maybe, he wanted to forget this part of his life. But perhaps these thoughts had been pent up for a long time.

Alvin kept watching for a fish to jump, but we didn't see any more. He leaned back on the bench.

       *   *   *

After basic training, I was assigned to a company that was training as a burial unit. We were told that this unit would stay together. We had one officer and three sergeants, all white. All the enlisted men were black. When I heard that, I knew who would get the dirty jobs. They tried to teach us how to plan a cemetery, how to layout grave sites, and how to arrange bodies. They kept telling us how important it was not to get dog tags mixed up. On field exercises we used dummies. The graves were not dug by hand but with a machine. The bodies were placed and covered up. Our job was not to run the machines, but to place the bodies in the right position. It didn't seem like it would be such a bad job. I even told my wife when I was home on leave that maybe I could work for the colored undertaker after I got out of the army. She didn't think much of my idea. I changed my mind after the war, too.

Well, like I said, after my second training I got leave to go home. As soon as I got back to Fort Lee, we got orders to ship out. That meant overseas, but we didn't know if it meant to Europe or to the Pacific. We went to Norfolk by train. We couldn't have passes or make phone calls, and we knew we would be on a ship in a few days. We just sat around the barracks waiting. Some of the boys played cards. I don't remember doing anything but eating and sleeping and going to a movie every night. We had formation every morning and had to police up the area.

On the third day, the orders came. We were to pack our bags, take a shower, put on clean clothes, write a letter home and give it to the sergeant to mail. That evening after supper, we were to bring our packed duffel bags to formation, ready to go.

After giving us loading instructions, the first sergeant said, "Are there any questions?"

One boy asked, "Sergeant, do you know where we're going?"

The sergeant answered quietly, "If I knew, I couldn't tell you, but I don't know and what difference does it make? If I were you I would worry about those submarines more than where you are going. We will be okay.

Our ship will be one of many in a convoy. The navy will get us where we're going."

It seemed we marched for miles with our heavy bags. It was almost dark, but I could see the camouflage paint on the ship as we came closer to it. The sailors were very nice and showed us where to go. There were six of us in a room with hammocks hung to sleep in. Having been on a fish boat each season for sixteen years, I sure didn't mind the ship. Some of the other men worried about seasickness and complained of the overcrowding, but I was in my element.

We could go on deck, but we were restricted to a certain area. We watched long lines of soldiers marching to the ship and coming on board. It reminded me of being on a fish boat in New York harbor. We saw big passenger ships coming into the harbor with people leaning over the railings, waving handkerchiefs and singing songs in a language we couldn't understand.

We were all excited when we heard the order to cast off lines. The ship, as well as the port, had no lights on except below deck. We were in a total black out area. From my place on deck, I could see the tugboats moving our ship. It wasn't long before they cast off their lines, and we were under our own power. Some of the men asked me how they could tell where they were going in the dark.

I said, "The pilot knows what he's doing. He's done this many times."

The sergeant suggested we get some sleep. He said when he got the schedule of meals he would let us know. Feeding all these people took a lot of planning. There was no moon, but we could hear ships all around us. I guess they were making up the convoy. I don't think any of us in our room slept good the first night. I know I didn't. I was up just before daybreak and saw them opening up the submarine net at the mouth of Chesapeake Bay. I could see the lighthouse at Cape Henry. I had seen that pretty sight many times. As day broke, I could see ships in all directions. It was a huge convoy.

I watched the lighthouse for as long as I could. I knew we were going to the east. I had heard a merchant marine seaman say one time that a convoy goes one direction and then another direction to throw off the enemy. Some other men came out on deck.

One of them asked, "What direction are we heading?"

I told him, "East right now, but that can change quickly."

"How do you know we're going east?" He said.

"See that ball of fire coming up out of the water? That's the sun, and it rises in the east. That's the way we're headin'."

About that time our sergeant came up and said, "Time for chow. We eat early. They told me there are eight shifts to eat and we are number two. We eat in the same order every meal."

Time passed slowly. When I was out on deck, I tried to count the ships, but I would come up with a different number every time. I didn't know much about the kinds of ships, but I could tell the freighters and the tankers. I had seen many of them up and down the coast when I was on the fish boat. The navy ships all looked alike. They all had guns on them. The only difference was some were bigger than others. We watched movies twice a day. I wasn't much interested, but I went. There wasn't much else to do.

On the third day, they had everybody come on deck and some big shot, some general or somebody, talked on the loud speaker. He told us we were going to Italy. We knew that the Allies had invaded Italy, but weren't making much progress. We didn't know then there would be another landing at Anzio, and we would be there.

Convoys move slowly. We'd been gone about a week when we hit a storm. It really wasn't too bad, but a lot of the boys got sick. The storm lasted the better part of two days. The worst part was the throw-up and the odor. I spent as much time on deck as I could and went to all the movies. Our sergeant told us it would be better after we got into the Mediterranean, and he was right. It was real rough going past the Rock of

Gibraltar, but once inside it was as smooth as the Chesapeake Bay on a hot summer day.

We soon found out our convoy was part of the invasion fleet that would go ashore at Anzio. They said we could expect air attacks at any time, so we had to wear our helmets except in bed. If an air attack was coming, there would be an alarm. There were meetings morning and night. We would be the last ones to go ashore. They showed us a map where our first cemetery would be. They knew a lot of people would be killed as they expected the Germans to defend the beach.

Now, time went fast, but our ship seemed to stand still. There were air raids several times a day, and we saw ships hit and some sunk. Finally, we went ashore. What a mess the beach area was: sunken landing crafts, parts of planes, and pieces of every kind of equipment. Some of it was burned, some was turned over, but some looked brand new. We met wounded men brought on stretchers from ambulances on their way to landing crafts that would take them to hospital ships. Once we were on shore our equipment came and together we went inland. I hadn't expected it to be cold in Italy in January, but it was very cold and windy. As we moved we could hear artillery fire. We also heard shells exploding and small arms fire. We saw anti-aircraft guns with mountains of empty shell cases near them. It wasn't until we got inland a little that we saw our job. Bodies were everywhere. They had been brought inland, up from the beach by field details and aid workers. We got our instructions and started on our first cemetery. None of us had ever experienced anything like this before. All the films and talks didn't prepare us for our job ahead. I was determined to do the best I could and give these poor boys a decent burial. Most of them were white, and so young. There were black bodies, too. We knew there were black combat units in the fighting. The hard part was trying to put pieces of the bodies together that belonged together. In some cases it was impossible. The air raids had been fierce and the artillery shelling, too, but our forces had secured a beachhead, and were moving inland. For the first several days we worked around the clock. I wasn't thinking too much about my safety. I just kept thinking about all these young boys whose lives were over. War was certainly horrible.

Sometimes I think about those boy's faces, those that had faces, during my first few days of burial duty in Italy. Our lieutenant told us we had a job to do and not to talk or think about "what if that was you lying there" or "your brother." He said, "You can't do anything about it, so try to think about something else. You'll get used to it." But I don't think anyone ever does. You just do your job. That's getting used to it, I guess. The lieutenant told us he had worked for an embalmer before he got drafted. One day he said, "Does anyone ever get used to death? I don't think I want to go back to that when this war is over."

As our forces continued to advance, we kept receiving more bodies. I heard one of the officers say that some of the cemeteries were temporary. A lot of the bodies would be shipped home; and the others, moved to a permanent cemetery. Our forces had captured Naples, and there was talk Rome would soon be taken.

You know, one of the hardest things for me when I came home was to face the Jim Crow laws. In Italy and later in France and Germany, we were treated just like white boys. It was hard to come back home and ride in the back of the bus.

Rome was the prettiest city I think I ever saw! I couldn't get over all those old buildings. I went to Rome three times. After working for a week or ten days we got a three-day pass. The first time I went, they gave us a tour of the city. A sergeant told us what each building was. Boy, it was beautiful! I don't know anything about Catholics, but they sure have pretty churches. If we ate in a restaurant they gave us wine with every meal. Food was scarce, but they sure did have good wine. I never got a headache the next day like I did at home. Some guy in my outfit told me it was the way they made it. It was really good.

As our forces took more and more of Italy, just one hill after another, we came across places where men in long robes lived and worked in old buildings. I think it had something to do with the church. They called these men monks. I saw the tower that leans that is really old. I don't understand why it doesn't fall over. They say it's been that way for hundreds of years. We finally came to a town called Florence where the Germans had blown up all the bridges except one. It was really old, with stores along each side of it as you crossed it. When we first got there the stores were empty, but they soon had things for sale. There were old churches there, too. One had carved doors of gold. I don't see how anybody could do that, but they sure did 'cause it was real. They called it "The Gates of Paradise."

I still think Rome was the prettiest. I had seen New York and Washington, but that Rome was something else. I liked the churches and the old brick walls best. But, that place where they had battles; men fighting men and men fighting animals, was the most interesting. I think it was called the Coliseum.

I went to France; saw Paris. I liked it, too, but I don't think the people were as friendly as they were in Italy. Maybe it was because I was black. The people didn't seem to like American blacks as much as the Italians did. Maybe the skin of the Italians is a little dark. I don't know.

Germany was really a mess. In some towns all the buildings were torn up, and the cities looked like battlefields. I felt sorry for those poor starving women and children. And I tell you a lot of us took stuff from our supply section and gave the people something to eat and blankets. Our sergeants and officers looked the other way. No one thought this was stealing. The people seemed nice enough, but they had nothing. When you compared what they had to the poorest blacks back home, the blacks at home were well off. As you heard me say before, we didn't have much, but we always had plenty of food and a roof over our heads.

*   *   *

I asked, "What do you think we got out of the war?"

"Well," he said, "we stopped Hitler and the Japs, but it didn't do us black people much good as far as Jim Crow laws at home. Our preacher was always

talking about becoming full citizens. The war brought us better jobs and more money than we ever had before. We had new fish boats in New Jersey and New York that were diesel. No more 'rolling coal.' Nice clean boats. They even painted them white."

Alvin looked out over the water and after a long pause said, "I still wake up nights and see those young bodies, men who died fighting that war."

CHAPTER 15

▼

CAP'N BILL LEE

One day I went by the store, and as I started up the steps, I met Alvin coming out with a bag of groceries in his arms. It was obvious he was walking since there were no other cars around, so I offered to take him home.

He accepted by saying, "I guess this bag would get heavy before I got home."

As he got out of the car, he invited me to take a seat under his pine tree and talk for a while. We sat down, and Alvin took a deep breath and looked around his yard. About this time his yellowish part-poodle dog, Gold Dust, came out from under a bush and started to scratch himself.

We talked about the slew of recent deaths in the community and how so many of the older people we had known were now gone.

"Who did you look up to when you were a child?" I asked.

"Well, I guess one man that I looked up to was Cap'n Bill Lee. He lived across the road from the farm where I grew up. I have heard the tale of his life so many times I'm not sure how much of it is true or how much of it has been changed, but I'll tell you how much of it I remember. I was nine years old

when he died. Black people talked about him a lot, and he was respected by black and white."

"What do you remember about him?"

*   *   *

It was said Bill Lee was a slave, who had been born in Maryland but was owned by a family down the road. The family had promised him he would-n't be separated from his wife and children; but they came on hard times and decided to sell Bill Lee. All the transportation at that time was either by horse or by boat. The market for the best slaves was farther south. That's what they told slaves, if they didn't behave, they'd be "sold south." Did you know my grandfather was a slave? Anyway, as the story goes, the steam-boats going south left from Merry Point in Lancaster County, near the Rappahannock River. Bill Lee was taken to Merry Point, given to an agent and shipped south. I remember him telling my parents that new cotton fields had opened up in Mississippi and more labor was needed. The land around here was worn out, and they didn't raise much cotton anymore. Down there new land was being cleared. It wasn't long before the war started. I remember Bill Lee sitting around our kitchen stove in the winter-time talking to Momma and Daddy about his life in Mississippi.

The man who owned him down there said when the war started there was no way the South could win. The North had too many people and too many factories. The South had too few people, too much cotton, and too many slaves. He said his owner wanted slaves to go into the Southern army. If they survived, they would get freedom for themselves and their families. He didn't think too many other slave owners shared his view because this was a white man's war, and no slaves went into the Southern army.

Bill Lee said he kept hearing that the fighting was getting closer. He fig-ured when the Yankees came, he would take off and head for home. When the Yankees got to northern Mississippi, his owner said the war was lost. It was about this time that news of the Emancipation Proclamation was heard in Mississippi. It spread like wildfire from plantation to plantation. He talked about how anxious he was to get back to Virginia and his family. He also talked about a time the Yankee soldiers came to the plantation trying to get the slaves to join them; telling them they were free to leave. Bill Lee said this was a white man's war, and the Negroes were being used by both sides. He said, "Let 'm fight! I just want to get back to Virginia and my family and be free. You turn all these slaves loose at one time, and there will be a mess. It just won't work. Most of the slaves ran off when the Yankees came. Some joined the Yankee army, but others just followed the army." He decided to leave, too, but he was going to work his way north to get to Virginia.

Daddy interrupted him and asked about his treatment as a slave in Mississippi. He said it wasn't much different from being a slave in Virginia. He also said he felt sorry for the free blacks. Most had no land and depended on the white landowners for jobs. They got the dirtiest and most dangerous jobs. If they got hurt, the landowner was not responsible. The slave owner had an investment in his slave and wanted to protect him. Bill Lee told us he was a foreman over other slaves and tried to get them the best care he could. Even so, he said slavery was evil. He didn't care what the Bible or anyone else said. No man had a right to own another person.

When he started to Virginia, he didn't know what army was where and didn't want to get caught by either. He didn't want to be put back into slavery by the Southern army or made a soldier in the Northern army. He just moved slowly north, staying near the rivers and streams, spending most of his time in the woods. He felt he could trust the black ex-slaves he came across who were roaming around like he was, but he wasn't roaming; he was different. He was heading toward home in Virginia. It took him more than two years to get to his family.

Bill Lee said he was sleeping in the woods one day, when a man threw a stick at him and woke him up. The man, who was white, had a gun.

"Where are you heading?" the man demanded.

"To Virginia!" Bill Lee answered.

"Well," he said, "I'm going to Maryland." The gun still pointed at him.

The man had tired of the army and had left. There was so much killing on both sides. He said he was in the Union Army and his brothers, two of them, were in the Confederate Army. His mother had written him they had been killed at Antietam. He had been at Vicksburg. He didn't know how many people he had killed, but no more. He said the whole war was silly. He wasn't fighting to end slavery or to keep anybody in the Union. Let them all go, he said. Enough was enough.

Bill Lee asked, "What part of Maryland are you from, Mister?"

"A tobacco farm south of Baltimore. Where are you from?"

"Virginia, on a farm between the Potomac and Rappahannock Rivers near the Chesapeake Bay."

"Well," the soldier said, "maybe we can travel together."

Bill Lee didn't feel like he had any choice. The man from Maryland, William Kelly, told him that after he had left the army, he had gone to a house to rob it. The only people there were a woman and two teenaged girls. The husband was in a prison camp in New York. When he asked the woman what she had, she said soldiers from both sides had taken all the horses, left them with one old cow, had tied the chickens together and hung them over their saddlebags. She said the Confederates were hungry, but the Yankees didn't need the food. They just didn't want it to fall into the hands of the Confederates. They took their swords and cut off the heads of the geese from horseback. Then they killed the pigs, leaving them to rot. She said she didn't know what they were going to eat that winter. She just hoped her husband got traded, but he hated the Yankees so much, she knew he would go right back in the army. William asked if they had any gold. The woman said "no." However, he noticed she had a gold ring on her finger. He told her to take it off. When he showed it to Bill Lee, he said, "That's all I got from them."

Bill Lee told him, "That was a bad thing to do."

"Don't worry," said the man from Maryland, "If I didn't get that ring, some other soldier would. They really picked those poor people clean. Don't tell me this war is over slavery. I have seen too much. I've even seen officers picking up bales of cotton and shipping it back up north. Not that they moved the cotton themselves, they got soldiers and Negroes to load it for them. Some of these officers are going to be rich when the war is over. Is this what we're fighting for? Not me, anymore! I had told my parents when the war was over, I was going to be a preacher, but now I just don't know."

Bill Lee said this white man helped him.

My father interrupted and said, "I bet you helped him too."

"Well," Bill Lee said, "just a little."

They tried to travel through areas that had not been torn up by the war, always going to the north. Once they came to a big plantation. They had to cross a creek in what William thought was Tennessee. Their plan was that Bill Lee would play William's slave and William would be the master. They cooked up the story that Bill Lee was being taken back to Kelly's plantation in Virginia. William Kelly, the white man, was the son of the plantation owner.

As they approached the house, William said, "Remember, let me do all the talking: let's don't forget our story."

William knocked at the front door, and an old man opened the door. The first thing Bill Lee noticed was the pistol in his hand. The second thing was that one of his shirtsleeves was empty. The one-armed man believed William's story. He told them all his slaves had run off, and he had no help. His wife was dead and his two sons were in the army somewhere in Virginia. William offered to help him by doing the cooking. He said Bill Lee would cut the wood and bring in water. William played his part well. He chained Bill Lee up at night not so he wouldn't run off, but because that's what a slave owner would have done. I guess they stayed there nearly a month. They helped the old man a whole lot and got fed and a change of clothes.

One day, three bounty hunters came riding up to the house looking for runaway slaves. They were about to ride off with Bill Lee when William pointed his gun at the leader and said, "That's my nigger! Take your hands off him! I've killed a lot of men in this war and one more won't make any difference. You take him, and you're dead. The rest of you might get me, but I'll get the first one that moves! Now get on out of here!"

They left, but William and Bill Lee could hear them talking to themselves, but couldn't understand what they were saying. The man with one arm came from behind a bush with his pistol in his hand and said, "I was going to take care of the other two. I don't know those men. Could be drifters from either side."

William thought they might come back, so he said they ought to leave right then. The man really hated to see them go, but he said he understood. He dug into his pocket and took out two one-dollar gold pieces. He gave them to William and thanked him for all his help.

By nightfall they were well on their way, carrying what food they had squirreled away. They traveled by night and slept in the woods in the day. William suggested they should keep their same story no matter who they met up with. Bill Lee says he hoped William knew which road to take because he sure didn't. They would watch the moon rise on the right and set on the left.

By then the nights were getting cold. The leaves had turned to their autumn colors and were falling. William said they needed to get through the mountains before winter or they would surely freeze. Their only other choice was to stay in the area until spring. One day they came to a river with a ferry tied up on their side. William had the idea to steal the ferry and go across to the other side. There was a rope tied on each side of the river that passed through a pulley on the ferry. When people crossed, they untied the ferry and pulled the rope by using a notched board so the rope wouldn't burn their hands. Just as Bill Lee and William started out, a man came running out of a shack near the shore and yelled, "You ain't taking my ferry!"

According to Bill Lee, William turned on the charm, told him the story, and explained how they needed to get home quickly. The man insisted they pay . . . twenty-five cents in silver or ten dollars in Confederate money. William pulled out one of the gold dollars and asked, "Will this be okay?"

The man looked at the coin, even bit it, then smiling wide, he said, "I don't have any change."

William said, "Okay," and kept on talking to him, asking how they could get through the mountains.

The ferryman said, "To try to cross the mountains on foot this time of year would almost surely mean death."

"Well, what can we do?"

Pulling at his chin whiskers, the ferryman said, "There's a cabin over there in the valley that's empty. The people done left with the war and all. You could stay there. You know, the Yankee boats are all over the big rivers bringing in supplies and hauling out cotton and anything else that's not nailed down."

William told him that's what they would have to do.

Bill Lee went on with his story telling us how he built traps and caught all kinds of animals and traded some for flour, salt, and matches. William had powder and shot in his pocket, but he tried to save those. They didn't have any money except the one gold dollar and the ring he had stolen off that poor woman in Mississippi. They stayed in the cabin until the end of March. By then the days were getting warmer, and the nights weren't too cold, so they started over the mountains. William talked to some of the local people and had a good idea about how it would be traveling, and what shape the roads were in. There were raiding parties out, coming in from the east and west, supposedly. They told William to stay out of the main traffic. When they started that leg of the trip, they were loaded down with food, but the load got light soon enough.

*   *   *

That day when Bill Lee was talking to my parents he leaned his chair back against the wall on two legs. My momma said, "Please don't break up our old furniture." He said he was sorry, but every time he talked about their journey over the mountains he got excited, thinking about how he felt knowing that every mile they went took them a mile closer to his family. He didn't know about his wife and children. He didn't know what was going on in Virginia, but he knew he was free.

*   *   *

One morning they heard horses on the road, but couldn't tell whether they were Union or Confederate. It was too dark to see their uniforms. They were the only people we saw on our trip through the mountains until we got in Virginia. William had relatives in Virginia, too. He said he knew the town they lived near, but had never seen them. He was going to tell them he was one of his brothers who was in the Confederate Army who was on his way back to his unit. He planned to tell that he had been a prisoner and had escaped.

*   *   *

"What did you do about food," Momma asked.

Bill Lee said, "You know I was a good trapper and knew a lot about the woods." He told us there was plenty of water in the streams, but they could still see snow on the high mountains. They ate a lot of rabbit and drank a lot of sassafras tea. They found poke and asparagus and honey the bears hadn't found and put it on cattail flour bread. They ate frog legs, boiled turtle and crawfish that reminded him of crabs at home. He felt like he was driven by the Lord. They were lucky to find nuts the squirrels had stored under rocks and in hollows. Once they were really short on food and William used his rifle to kill a deer even though they knew the sound would travel a long way. As soon as they could get to that deer they made tracks! By the time they got through the mountains they were tired and hungry and weak.

Bill Lee interrupted his story and said, "Man! What would I have given for a pan of cornbread like you have sitting on the table there."

*   *   *

After they got into the valley, William was sure they were in Virginia. He said the first town they came to he would go to try to find out where they were and what the war situation was. When they got to the town, William told Bill Lee to stay by a certain tree in the woods on the edge of town where he could find him again.

When William came back, he said he had talked to an old man who told him most of the food had either been burned or carried off by one side or the other. The man said most everyone was hungry, but the word was out that the war would soon be over. The Confederates were holding a line between Richmond and Petersburg, but with the spring campaign, it might end. People were saying the South was defeated but not conquered. The old man also told him Yankee raiders still came often. They didn't want any supplies going to the Confederates.

Truth was, by that time there was nothing left to feed the people there. Some of the people farther up the valley had moved into Pennsylvania. Their homes, barns, stock and fields had been destroyed. There were deserters from both sides everywhere trying to get home. For them the war was over.

William turned to Bill Lee and said, "I am one of many."

They had to move on up the valley. They used their wits to get home, staying off the roads and moving mainly at night. He said they heard very few barking dogs. I guess the people were real hungry. They ate off the land same as when they were coming over the mountains. William spent a lot of time scouting around to see which way they should go. They made good time. The weather was clear, warm in the daytime and not cold at night. Spring was almost upon them. I guess they were just glad to be alive and going home.

The story has it that William came back excited one evening. He had come upon a rebel deserter on his way home and had gotten the draw on him. That deserter told William the rebels were barely holding out at Petersburg. They were starving. One battle would probably drive them out of their trenches. He said he had had enough and was going home to his family. He knew they were hungry, too. The deserter told William he was sure the war would soon be over. This made William want to get back in a unit so he wouldn't be charged with desertion. He said, "Maybe I can claim to have been a prisoner."

As the days got longer, Bill Lee and his traveling partner, William, got more excited each day. All of the part of Virginia they were in was controlled by Union forces by that time. The land was flat, so William said it was time to head east, and before long they crossed a stream.

William said, "This is the beginning of the Rappahannock River."

Bill Lee replied, "This little stream sure don't look like the same big Rappahannock River I was on when I was sold south."

The next day they heard the war was over. This news really worried William. He decided they needed to stay put in the woods and start putting some food aside for their separate journeys.

They stayed near there for a while. On one of Bill Lee's "looks around" he came across a makeshift cemetery and saw an old man digging. He would dig a while and then sit down to rest. Bill Lee stayed still in the woods watching him, but he must have moved 'cause the old man saw him and called to him to come there. Bill Lee says he was sure scared! Scared to go and scared to run! After a moment though, he walked over to the man slowly. Bill Lee thought he might have a gun.

The old man said, "I've come more than a hundred miles in an ox cart for my only son's body. He died of wounds he got at the Battle of the Wilderness and was buried here. I'm worn out from traveling and grief.

Everything at home is torn up with so many killed and wounded. We have almost nothing to eat."

"Where are you from?" Bill Lee asked.

The man said his name was Snow and he had come from Northumberland County. Bill Lee knew this was his way to get home. He told Mr. Snow his story about how William and he had been traveling together. He left out which side William had fought for.

The old man asked Bill Lee if he would help him, then they could travel together. Bill Lee agreed at once and took the worn shovel. He started to dig, and before long they had the body loaded on the ox cart. The oxen were tied to a tree in the shade and were lying down chewing their cud. They were so poor, Bill Lee didn't see how they could pull an ox cart a hundred miles. He knew for certain he would have to walk.

Bill Lee found William near a stream about a hundred yards away and told him about Mr. Snow and the chance to get home. William shook Bill Lee's hand saying how much he had done for him. He said Bill Lee had sure kept him alive, but Bill Lee said, "It worked both ways. We were a good team. What are you going to do?"

William smiled, "I'll think up a good lie and get by with it."

With that they said goodbye.

*　　　　　　*　　　　　　*

"Well," I said, "Alvin, that is quite a story. I know it's generally true because I've heard parts of it from Cap'n Bill's grandchildren, too. What happened after he got home?"

"All I remember," said Alvin, "is what my parents told me. I used to keep the cemetery clean where he is buried. I remember his tombstone said he was born in 1830 and died in 1922. He came back home, found his family again, and somehow got a sailboat and hauled freight to Baltimore. He brought supplies back to this area on his return trip. At one time he even had a mail contract and brought mail from Baltimore to Coan Wharf. He built a house on *his farm on Surprise Hill where his granddaughter had the funeral home, and he was active in the founding of Shiloh Church. Everybody, both black and white, called him 'Cap'n Bill.'*

"Thanks for the story, Alvin, I've heard my mother say he brought freight to my grandfather's store right down the road. He must have been some man. I sure would like to hear more, but I'd better go now. My wife says I go and take my mouth and don't know when to come home."

CHAPTER 16

▼

ALVIN'S HEROES

It was several days before I got another chance to talk to Alvin. As I drove into his driveway, he was sitting in his usual chair in the yard under the shade of his pine tree. It was a warm October day. The trees in the nearby woods had begun to turn. The colors were beautiful, deep scarlet, bright yellow and orange-red, the colors of sunrise over the bay. What a beautiful day, I thought.

As I approached Alvin and we exchanged greetings, I noticed his voice had taken on a sense of urgency. He said, "I have been thinking about a lot of things, people, too, and I want to tell you before I forget. If you want to know people I knew when I was growing up, I need to talk while things are fresh in my mind. You know, us old folks soon forget. I want to tell you while I still remember.

"Okay, Alvin," I said, "tell me everything. I'm glad of the chance to listen."

"You know my mother worked for Miss Linda Covington, and she had all kinds of meetings at her house. My mother would serve cake and tea to the ladies. One organization that met there was the U.D.C."

"You mean the United Daughters of the Confederacy?'

"Yeah, I guess that's right. Momma was always concerned that they would want to put blacks back into slavery, but Miss Linda told her it was only to promote the heroes of the Civil War and to decorate their graves and to help look out for widows and orphans of veterans."

I interrupted him saying, "You mean Southern veterans?"

"Yeah, that's it. Anyway, one day Momma came home talking about how your mother wouldn't join although her mother and her sister were members. Your mother is said to have said, 'No sir.' I remember so well what Momma said your mother's reason was. She said the Civil War was caused by hot heads on both sides and should never have happened. Momma said, 'Now there's a white woman who says what's on her mind.' Do you remember the heads of generals Miss Linda had in the front hall?"

"Oh yes, Alvin," I said. "I remember the marble busts of Lee and Jackson sitting on pedestals that were taller than I was as a little boy, and I was scared of them! They looked so real!"

Alvin leaned back in his chair and nearly fell over. As he righted himself, he said, "Those people may be heroes to some and maybe they were good generals, but my heroes are people like my neighbor, Mrs. Williams."

"You mean Aunt Dinks?" I asked.

"Yeah, that's right, she raised her own family and raised her daughter's son after his mother died. Also, another daughter and her girl lived with her. The girl couldn't go to school because she was crippled and walked with a crutch. You know, teachers came almost every day after school to teach this girl. Now she works in some office in Baltimore. She's done real good, I hear. And the boy finished high school, too. Do you know how Mrs. Williams made a living?"

I didn't get a chance to answer.

"She did some housework for people and took in wash. People would bring her baskets of dirty clothes to wash and iron. She did a lot of this ironing at night, but, you know, she didn't have running water in the house. She would have to go to the well, lower a bucket, pull it up, carry it to the house, put it in a big kettle on her stove and heat it. She also had to heat the irons on the stove. She kept two irons heating while she used one. To me this is what makes a hero, somebody who does something for somebody else. You remember, too, she was deaf. She was taken sick with the mumps in childhood and was left completely deaf."

I broke in and said, "Sure, I remember. She sure could read lips. She knew everything you said. You could tell she was smart. She must have taught herself."

Alvin seemed more relaxed. He kind of smiled and said, "Do you remember Ol' Man James Conway? Lived down on the old road going to Fairport? He had been a slave, got sold as a young man for seven pieces of silver to some place near Richmond. He spent seven or eight years there. After the war he came home and raised a nice family. He was a hard worker, but it wasn't easy. If you think the whites were poor, the blacks had nothing. My grandfather was also a slave and went through the same kind of thing."

Alvin's talking brought to mind the time I went as a child with my father to hire some men for his crew on the boat. He couldn't find anyone home that Sunday afternoon. Finally, a child at one house told us that everybody had gone to the baptism down at Merry Point near the ferry dock. By the time we arrived, several hundred black people had gathered. My father soon found the minister. As it turned out, he had known him from his childhood. The minister's father had been a slave on my great-grandfather's farm. On the way home, my father told me that after the Civil War was over, the minister's family didn't want to leave the farm that was their home. My great-grandfather and the minister's father made a deal. They agreed on wages and the family continued to live in the old slave quarters. He worked on the farm in the summer and caught oysters in the winter. My father and his old friend talked about hunting and fishing, waving their hands high in the air to mimic geese flying or the length of fish caught. After World War I, my father and his brother tore down the old slave quarters which was then being used for storage.

Alvin and I both got up and stretched. My back was stiff and raising my arms made it feel better. As I stood there I thought about Bill and Fred Cooper and Christopher Lee. I had played with all of them as a child. I mentioned them to Alvin.

"Yeah, those boys have done good," said Alvin.

I went on, "When I started to school, I road a bus, but these kids and other black children had to walk to their school. I didn't understand, but I was told there wasn't enough money for buses for everybody. People said the whites owned most of the land and paid most of the taxes, so they got the buses. But it didn't seem right. When I got older I questioned the separate but equal doctrine. It wasn't until after I was in the second or third grade that black children got buses.

"I remember the last time I saw Bill Cooper. I was a freshman at the Medical College of Virginia Dental School and Bill was the first black to enter the MCV Pharmacy School. I was walking down Broad Street with my wife at noon one day and we met Bill. He and I recognized each other and greeted each other with a big hug. I don't think any of the other people around knew what to think when they saw a white man hugging a black man on the streets of Richmond in 1956. Well, we hadn't seen each other for years. You know Fred, Bill's brother, and Christopher Lee both became teachers, and, I think, principals. They and their families worked and saved every penny they could. They thought education was their key to success."

I looked Alvin in the eye, "Boy, we could sure use more of that attitude today."

Alvin nodded his agreement.

I had enjoyed talking about past times and old friends. I said, "Alvin, I'm going to the fish dock in the next day or two and I'll bring you some fresh fish."

Alvin grinned and said, "Nothing like nice fresh fish."

As I said goodbye, I got in the car, drove around his circular drive and hit the horn as I left the driveway.

As I came down the road I looked over at Charles Toulson's house. This black man had built his own house and the houses of four of his children on adjoining lots. He not only built the houses, he went into his woods and cut the logs and sawed the logs into lumber. Another time I remember him building a workboat in his yard.

Wheat threshing
(courtesy of F.A. Pazandak Photographic Collection NDIRS-NDSU)

Charles Toulson couldn't read or write. When I was a child he took his thrashing machine from farm to farm to thrash the grain that had been cut by a binder pulled by horses. The binder tied the bundles that were then stacked in shocks. After drying, the bundles were loaded on wagons with a pitchfork and carried to the thrashing machine that was powered by a belt from a tractor. I loved to watch the auger push out the grain be it wheat, barley, oats, or rye that was caught in wooden half-bushel measures and dumped into bags. At five or six years old I was delighted to help hold the bags. The farmers nearby brought their horses and wagons to help. They, too, would get their grain thrashed with help of neighbors. The straw was thrown high in the air through a long chute which could be raised as the straw stack got larger. The straw stack was really fun to play on.

I was always amazed how a man could cut and remove the twine on each bundle as it was laid on the thrashing table, shoving it into the teeth of the machine all with one motion. This was usually done by Charles Toulson's oldest son, Eunice.

Later, Eunice was an engineer on a menhaden fishing boat. He worked as second engineer on a boat my father captained. The chief engineer had quite a problem with drinking on weekends and wasn't ever able to work on Mondays, usually the best fishing day since the fish had an extra day to "school up." The owner of the boat would not let the black man take the boat out. In the end they solved the problem by getting the chief engineer up to start the engine and leave the dock. Then the chief engineer would go back to bed, and Eunice would run the boat.

As I turned to go up the road, I passed Nathan White's house. He had been a drive boatsman on the boat with my father. As a child I went out fishing with them sometimes. When they made a set I would go with him in the drive boat. His job was to row the boat to the other side of the school of fish and drive them into the spreading purse net which was let out from two purse boats lowered into the water from the larger boat. He rowed standing up and waved an oar in the direction the school of fish was moving. My father had the utmost confidence in him, not just in his ability to do his job, but in his ability to look out for me, in sometimes hazardous conditions.

I remember years later I was in the bank to make a deposit. Nathan was at the window ahead of me. He had a handful of checks and was trying to make a deposit. I was sure it was for a large amount of money as he was one of the top menhaden captains on the Gulf of Mexico that year. I knew the teller was new to the area and I could see she was hesitant about taking the deposit. I walked up to Nathan and I told him I'd heard he'd had a great season. He was glad to see me. Then I turned to the lady at the window and explained who he was. She readily accepted his deposit.

I had known Nathan's mother and father and most of his brothers and sisters. As a child, I used to love to ride my bicycle to their house to talk to his mother and look at the animals and their garden. Once my mother had engaged a goose from his mother for Thanksgiving. After she had dressed it and had it in a pan, I went on my bicycle to pick it up.

Nathan's mother exclaimed, "How in this world are you going to get home on your bicycle with that goose?"

I said I was going to carry the goose in the pan under my arm, but we finally decided to put the pan with the goose in it in my carrier and tie it down. She told me to come back after I got the goose home and tell her how I made out. Thanks to her, I made out fine with the goose.

It is a tradition in Tidewater Virginia to have oysters for the holidays. One Christmas while I was in the army, my mother acquired some oysters in the shell. My father was dead and neither she nor my sister could shuck them. She had tried to hire several different people who came into the post office where she worked to shuck them for her, but she had no takers. When Captain Nathan White came in, she asked if he knew anyone she could hire. He said he had to go home for a minute but he would be glad to come back and shuck them for her. He did it at no charge.

CHAPTER 17

▼

THE BANK

On my next visit to Alvin I decided to ask him what he remembered of the bank robbery in Reedville. I knew he would have been old enough to remember it, and everybody talked about it then. The bank was robbed and burned in 1921, and the president of the bank was convicted and sent to prison for a while.

When I asked Alvin about it, he smiled and said, "My daddy had a little of his tomato money in it. That was his only cash crop, you know, and the money was what he had left of it. It was February, a bad time to lose any money, since there was nothing coming in. He never got any money back, even though they found some of the money that was stolen.

"The pilot on the menhaden fishing boat that I was on for several seasons was one of the young boys who found about $20,000 under the church steps while he was at a funeral with his mother. The boys were playing around the steps after the funeral while their parents were talking and found a bag with the money in it."

"Alvin, I read the newspaper account of the robbery, and he wasn't listed as one of the ones who found the money, but I've heard him say he found the bag first," I said.

Alvin went on, "Every time he had a few drinks he would sit in the galley and talk about finding the money. He would shake his head, and say, 'How dumb I was to turn that money in. The money was unmarked and couldn't be traced. None of the money ever got back to the depositors. The bank was broke.' He would say over and over again, 'What a fool I was for turning in the money.' Of course, everybody knew it was only the liquor talking. He wouldn't take something that wasn't his. He would say, 'What would you have done?' We always told him he did the right thing. It never came up unless he was drinking."

I said, "Some of the bricks from the burned bank were hauled to the house next door to us to replace the porch floor. Concrete was poured on top of the bricks and it made a nice place for us kids to roller skate, since we had no sidewalks. The other bank in Reedville sure had an interesting story, too, didn't it, Alvin?"

"Yep, it sure did! I know a little about it, but I'm sure you know more. So you tell me," Alvin said.

"Well, it was during the depression. The government closed the banks and called it a bank holiday. I think it was 1934. The only banks that were going to be allowed to reopen were the ones in sound condition. This did not include the bank in Reedville. One of the directors of the bank, a man named Captain Fisher, an eighty-five-year-old sea captain, said he would put up his own money for the bank to reopen. He and his brother-in-law had at one time owned a large menhaden processing plant. The bank examiners said he must be crazy. No one could or would do that. Captain Fisher said, 'You'll see.'

"The officers of the bank went to Washington to tell the banking regulators they had a man who was going to put up the money for them to reopen. They were laughed at and told to go home and get the story straight.

"In the meantime, Captain Fisher, driven by his chauffeur with an armed man riding 'shotgun,' went to his bank in New Jersey and got the necessary $120,000 in cash, in a satchel and held the satchel between his feet all the way home. When he got to Reedville he found the bank officers had returned from Washington and had been laughed at. Captain Fisher turned right around and went to Washington. When he entered the regulator's office he slapped his cane on the desk a few times, and said in sea captain's language, 'You *so and sos* didn't think Fisher would come through!'

"They told him even with his loan the bank wouldn't be able to pay interest and pay off the loan. He said he didn't care. He had made his money in Reedville and this was his way of paying some of it back. He did not want any interest, and they could take as long as they needed to pay it back. He said, 'If I die before they can pay it back, they can pay my heirs.' And that's what happened. Alvin, could you imagine anybody doing that today?"

Alvin replied, "I sure can't!"

It was about time to feed my cows, so I said goodbye and told him I would be back soon.

Chapter 18

▼

Goodbye

I didn't know it at the time, but this would be my last talk with Alvin. He looked well and seemed to be in a good mood as he sat in his chair under the pine tree. It was a bright pleasant October afternoon. The sky was clear except for a few cumulus clouds, rolling from west to east. We exchanged our greetings and I petted Gold Dust who kept smelling my pant legs, sniffing the scent of my own dogs.

I said, "Alvin, there are a lot of things I'd like to ask you. One of them is about your uncle."

"You mean my Uncle Jim who got killed in 1937?" he said.

I nodded my head.

"Well, he lived about a half a mile up the road, and had a cleaning business. His wife was dead. When he died it was late winter, but the snow was still on the ground, and it was cold. Uncle Jim's wife's brother, Richard, stayed with him and helped in the cleaning business. One night Uncle Jim's house burned to the ground. Next morning, Richard was standing around the smoldering ruins. Everyone asked where Jim was, and Richard kept saying he didn't know. He said he had stayed with a sister of his the night before and had come back to the house that morning. Part of the remains of Uncle Jim's body was soon found in the ashes of his house, the rest were down his well. Uncle Jim was quite a worker and had a large cleaning business for that time and was thought to have stashed away some money. If there was anyone who held a grudge against him, my family sure didn't know about it. He was such a kind and gentle man.

"The sheriff had an idea that Richard was the one who killed him, but there was no proof. Every time the sheriff questioned Richard he knew nothing, although it was known they had had an argument. Richard wanted to raise baby chickens in Jim's house. Uncle Jim wouldn't let him do it."

I told Alvin, when I was a child, I remember Richard coming to the post office every day waiting for the mail. My mother was postmaster, and I spent a lot of time hanging around the post office. Every day Richard said this would be the day he would get his bonus check for military service in World War I. I was eight years old, so I didn't know what he was talking about, but as I remember, he was always very nice to me.

The post office was in an old store that had been a general store run first by my great grandfather, then by my grandfather. Most of the country stores at that time had a front porch where the loafers passed time. One time a local farmer had a load of watermelons he couldn't sell. My father bought them for me to sell on the old store porch. Richard helped me sell the melons to people coming to the post office for their mail. One of the most prominent businessmen in the area who always made a lot of me came by. When I asked him to buy a melon, he said, "I'm on my way home for lunch, but I will stop on the way back to my office."

"The price will go up at noon," I told him.

With a smile he said, "I can't compete with such a good businessman," and he bought several melons.

Richard said, "That was a good sale."

Every now and then we would cut a melon and give pieces to those who were hanging around. I thought Richard was great, so I couldn't imagine him killing anyone.

Alvin went on with his story. "The sheriff questioned Richard every day. Finally, Richard said, "If you get me a bottle of liquor, I'll tell you everything I know about Jim's death."

"The sheriff thought it might help. Anyway it was worth a try. At that time there were no liquor stores in the county so he had to drive to another county to buy the liquor. He said he sure wasn't going to any bootlegger in the county, although he knew plenty and had arrested most of them several times. When he came back, he gave the bottle to Richard hoping for some word that might help him solve the crime. Richard slowly drank all of the liquor in the bottle. Then the sheriff began asking him questions. Richard looked at the sheriff with glassy eyes and slurred speech and said, 'I done told you where I was that night.' Then he passed out. After he slept it off, the sheriff told him he had better leave the county and not come back. There was never any arrest and there never was any trial."

Alvin added slowly, "We never found out who killed Uncle Jim, but somebody sure did. For a long time I would wake up nights thinking about what happened to Uncle Jim. Later, in the war, I saw the terrible things people could do to each other."

*   *   *

"Alvin, as I was coming up the road, I noticed they were taking down that big old oak tree where Uncle Henderson Locust used to live. I remember sitting under that tree with him, listening to him talk about tending sheep as a slave boy. He was always interested in talking about old times, not unlike what we're doing.

Alvin smiled, "Did you know about the big poker game?"

"No," I said, "Please tell me about it."

"Usually the bets were small, but on this day they got out of hand."

"Were you there, Alvin?" I asked.

"I was there at John's house when the big bet was made. The two men left in the game each thought they had a winning hand and went crazy betting. One of the fellows ran out of money, so he put up the tree to cover his bet. When his bet was called, each had a full house, one had five tens, and the other had five fives."

"Wait a minute, Alvin, that's impossible!" I said.

Alvin grinned and said, "I didn't tell you the twos were wild. The new owner of the tree has two sons living away. He decided to take down the tree and give the sons the wood to burn in their fireplaces. Nobody had a power saw big enough to take down the tree trunk. So they decided to go up the tree about forty feet where the limbs began and cut each of them. They counted more than one hundred growth rings in those limbs."

I was amazed and said, "Alvin, that sure is an old tree. I wonder how many rings would be in the trunk of the tree. Each ring represents a year of growth, you know."

Even today the dead trunk remains standing and I think about it every time I pass it. It was sad to see the old tree die.

Several days later I heard that Alvin had suffered a stroke and was in the hospital. I called his wife, Myrtle, several times to inquire about him. She suggested I go to see him, so I did. When I went in his room, he was tied in a chair looking off into space. I tried to talk to him, but he couldn't respond. A day or two later I got a call telling me that Alvin "Stack" Wormley had died.

Remains of the old oak tree (courtesy of Mike Domas)

About the Author

▼

John H. Harding, Jr. was born in Northumberland County, Virginia. He attended local schools, graduated from the College of William and Mary and taught school one year before serving two years in the army. In 1960 he graduated from the Medical College of Virginia, School of Dentistry, returned to Northumberland County where he practiced for thirty-one years.

After retirement he published his first book, *Shortchanged*, about a boyhood friend who was killed in Korea. The book was endorsed by the Korean War Veterans Association and the Honorable John O. Marsh, Jr., former secretary of the army.